DATE			

THE CRYSTAL GARDEN

THE
CRYSTAL GARDEN

Vicki Grove

031951

G. P. Putnam's Sons ⬥ New York

G. P. Putnam's Sons, a division of The Putnam & Grosset Group,
200 Madison Avenue, New York, NY 10016. G. P. Putnam's Sons,
Reg. U.S. Pat. & Tm. Off. Published simultaneously in Canada.
Printed in the United States of America.
Designed by Gunta Alexander and Sue H. Ng.
Text set in Horley Old Style.
Library of Congress Cataloging-in-Publication Data
Grove, Vicki.   The crystal garden / Vicki Grove.   p.   cm.
    Summary: Looking for a new beginning after her father's death, Eliza
and her mother move to a backwater town in Missouri where Eliza's
desperate attempts to be popular in her new school are thwarted
by her growing friendship with the eccentric girl next door.
    [1. Friendship—Fiction. 2. Popularity—Fiction. 3. Schools—
Fiction. 4. Mothers and daughters—Fiction. 5. Death—Fiction.]
    I. Title. PZ7.G9275Cr 1994 [Fic]—dc20 94-32702 CIP AC
ISBN 0-399-21813-0
10 9 8 7 6 5 4 3 2 1 First Impression

To J.D.,
my sapphire

CHAPTER
~1~

Last spring my mother's boyfriend, Burl Hawkins, quit his real job at Sears and moved down south to the Ozarks to play full-time with his country western band, the Tuscumbia Heartbreakers. Then three months later, right out of the blue, he came back to Kansas City to talk my mother into moving down there with him. To be honest, she'd warned me he might do that, but you also might get hit by a bus at any second and you don't worry a whole lot about it till it happens.

I saw Burl before Mama did that sticky August day he came back. I was sitting on the steps of our apartment building with Mr. Amos, our building custodian. Usually we would have been playing gin rummy, but that day we were trading baseball cards when this pickup came barreling down Troost Avenue and jerked to a halt right in front of us with one tire clear up on the curb. The door swung open and out got Burl, carefully as a butterfly emerging from an ugly old cocoon. Except for the truck he was completely changed, head to toe—or I should say, hat to boots.

He just stood there on the sidewalk grinning and glittering, waiting for us to get a good long look.

"Why Burl Harley Hawkins, I reckon I need my sunglasses to look at you directly!" Mr. Amos cackled.

"Burl!" I jumped to my feet, too astounded by the look of him to even feel worried yet about his being back. "Where'd you get the clothes?"

His shirt was red on the top and sleeves, with rhinestones outlining each pocket, and gold cord running down to fancy sharp points above his stomach. Beneath the points the shirt was turquoise, with more rhinestones here and there. His jeans were red too, almost purple. He had on these glove things that came halfway up his arms, with fringe along the sides, and his belt had a silver buckle with a horse's head engraved in it. The horse had a huge ruby eye.

"So, you like the outfit," Burl said, though neither Mr. Amos nor I had told him any such thing. He strutted slowly around to show off the back of his shirt. There was a picture of a huge heart, in two pieces. Down the middle "Tuscumbia Heartbreakers" was embroidered in some kind of shiny, sequiny red writing.

"Wow," I said. "Did all seven of you Heartbreakers get an outfit like that?"

"Yup, as a matter of fact we did, Eliza Marie, and it cost us a small fortune," Burl said proudly. "Put it on the old MasterCard."

Mr. Amos had by then struggled to his feet and walked over to run his long, papery fingers over the horse's eye.

"My, my," he said in a quiet, breathless way.

Burl touched the brim of his hat like the good guys in cowboy movies do when they walk past the women. Or past the old men, like Mr. Amos.

"Much obliged," Burl said, as if Mr. Amos had complimented him. He gave us each a wink, then walked on up the stairs and disappeared inside the building.

"Mama's not home," I whispered to Mr. Amos. "She's at Winstead's." I knew Burl was the one I should be telling that to, but I didn't go after him. He'd find out for himself when he made it up our five flights of stairs.

"My, my," Mr. Amos said again. This time he shook his head slowly, and moved the sides of his mouth downward in puzzlement. "What's the world come to, Eliza?" he asked, turning to frown at me like he expected a real answer.

How was I supposed to know what the world had come to? I shrugged.

"Didja get a load of his boots?" Mr. Amos whispered.

I shook my head. My eyes had been too dazzled by the top half of Burl to get down that far.

"Red at the heels, red at the toes," Mr. Amos said. "Guitars stitched up the sides."

"I better go tell Mama that Burl's here," I muttered. I jumped the bottom three steps and ran full-speed down the street.

◆ ◆ ◆

3

It was a five-block run to Winstead's, then I slowed down to squeeze past the cars nosed into the parking spaces around the restaurant. Mama wasn't a carhop. She was the only grown-up waitress, so she worked inside and left the carhopping to the high-school girls who worked part-time.

I was through the heavy front doors and sliding onto a stool at the counter before I noticed that Cindy Jenkins and Pammy Hirsch and a bunch of their friends were sitting in the big round booth in the corner. Normally I would have checked for that sort of thing before I came in. I would have hid behind the Dumpster in the parking lot and peered through the big plate glass window that ran all around the front of the building until I was sure nobody from school was there. But that day my mind was on Burl.

"Hi, Eliza." Chuck, the manager, turned partway toward me. He was reading the little green pages the waitresses had stuck in the order holder. "I'll tell your mom you're here."

"No, don't!" I glanced over my shoulder. None of the girls in the corner had noticed me—yet.

Chuck glanced at the girls too, then, smiling and frowning at the same time. "Some of your friends from sixth grade?"

I slid off the stool. "I've got to go home," I whispered. "I'll talk to Mama tonight, after her shift."

I pretended to study the row of gumball machines by the doors on my way out, keeping my face turned away from the booth in the corner. When I was finally safely

4

outside in the parking lot, I stood for a few seconds hidden behind the Dumpster, watching.

I saw Mama go over to the round corner booth, smiling and chattering away. She even stooped over to wipe off their table, like she was their slave or something. Cindy and Pammy and the others studied the menus she handed around without having to even check in their purses to see if they had any money.

♦　♦　♦

Burl's ugly truck was still there when I got back to our block. Mr. Amos was gone, probably to collect somebody's rent or to repair somebody's toilet. I reluctantly went up the concrete stairs and on into the shadowy lobby, and there was Burl, bending over the table where the mailman always put the junk mail that was too big for our box. He was staring upward into the little mirror Mr. Amos had hung to cover up a hole in the plaster. His hat was on the table, balanced on a pile of old grocery-store fliers.

"Excuse me," I mumbled, flustered, and hurried toward the stairs that would get me to our apartment.

"Say, little missy," Burl called, "come and looky here for just one second, could you? I'd appreciate your opinion."

I stopped and slouched against the wall, one foot on the bottom stair. "What?"

Burl turned toward me, still hunched over, his fingers in the few thin orange hairs that grew in a clump just behind his forehead.

5

"Think a hair transplant would help?" he asked. "Answer me honest, now. Them suckers'll cost you upwards of ten thousand bucks, but it'd be worth it if it would truly help."

"Help what?" I knew he was almost bald, of course. I guess what I was really asking was, since he'd been almost bald all along, why was he worried about it now?

"Help my image," he answered. "Image is important in my new life, playing with the band full-time."

He took his fingers from his hair and picked up his hat. He stared at it, sliding his fingers nervously along the brim, back and forth. I guess right about then I knew for sure what was coming.

"Eliza?" he said after a few seconds, putting on the hat and at the same time putting a little sad gruffness into his voice. "You know, it was an awful tragedy that took your daddy, but that's been near three years ago. I guess I see this move to the Ozarks as an opportunity for a fresh start, not just for me but for you as well. That is, I see it as a chance for both you and your mama and me to pool our resources and make a run for what we really want. You understand?"

"No," I replied, thinking that Mama and me and him didn't make a "both." Mama and me were a both, without him.

My eyes flickered toward his eyes, then flickered away. I stared instead into the fake ruby eye of the horse on his fancy belt buckle. "You're here to talk Mama into moving, right?" I said.

I wasn't really even smiling, but Burl looked so relieved and cheerful you'd have thought I was jumping for joy and acting like I loved the idea. He stuck his thumbs into his belt loops and threw his shoulders back a little. His stomach slid out farther so it partly covered the belt-buckle horse's ears.

"Eliza, I'm proud to say I've got a place all fixed up for us. I've managed to purchase a lot, complete with a renovated mobile home, in a resort town not more'n half an hour west of downtown Branson, the new country music capital of the USA, if not almost practically the entire world!"

"What's the name of the town?"

"Well, it's a real historical town, named after the wounded Civil War veteran who carved it from the lush wilderness. Or actually, named after the wound that valiant hero received."

"What's the name exactly?"

"Gouge Eye," Burl said. "Your new home, girl, will be in the small city of Gouge Eye, Missouri, population 438, counting the three of us."

◆ ◆ ◆

Mama and I stood silently at the sink that night, making dinner while Burl watched TV in our living room. "Penny for your thoughts," she finally said, softly. She nudged me with her hip, but I moved a couple of inches away and didn't bump back.

"Oh now, come on, hon," she said, sliding over a couple of inches to bridge the gap between us and tickling

7

at my ribs with her elbow. "You can't be that shocked. I mean, sweetie, I told you if Burl could get a toehold in the Ozarks he'd most likely ask us to share it with him."

"But Mama, why can't he just play down in Branson with his band, but live up here in Kansas City like he did before, when he was playing part-time and working at Sears?"

"Shhh! Honey, he'll hear you, okay?" She cocked her head, listening, but Burl let out a moan that told us he was paying attention to the wrestling on TV, not to our conversation. Mama smiled, and kissed me quickly on the forehead. "Because he plays more like full-time now and lives in Gouge Eye, Eliza. His house is over a hundred thirty miles away from here." She pushed a strand of curly red hair from her forehead with the back of her hand. Her eyes were bright as she let a long curl of potato skin fall into the sink.

"It's not a house, it's a trailer," I murmured. "The only reason to have trailers is so you can move them when you want to."

"Oh, Lize, you can't move a big old thing like that along Highway Seventy-one back and forth, there to here, whenever you get the urge." She looked at me, and a long curl fell back over her eye. "Liza? Would you really want Burl to give up his musical dreams to work as a parts man at the Sears garage the rest of his life?"

I was dying to point out the obvious, that Burl just wasn't that hot a guitar player in the first place, and that dreams were pretty stupid if you didn't have the stuff to back them up.

But I didn't say that, of course, because I'm not rude. Besides, I was sick of talking around the edges of things. I wanted us to get to the point.

"But you don't love Burl," I whispered, staring right into her eyes. "So why should we go with him?"

She opened her mouth slightly, took in a quick little breath of air, and just looked back at me for a few long seconds. Finally she swallowed, turned toward the sink, and pressed both her hands against its porcelain edge. She looked down at the pile of potato skins.

"Eliza, I am so tired," she said in a flat, gray voice I'd never heard her use before. "I have just got to take a chance on some other kind of life for us. Some new life, away from all the . . . the memories here." She straightened her shoulders then, and she was smiling when she turned back toward me. "Besides, hon, I'm fond of Burl. He makes me laugh again. He makes me think things just might change for the better."

I was thinking that things could also change for the worse, especially if you pick a town with a name like Gouge Eye for a so-called "new life."

CHAPTER

—2—

Sometimes I'm just too polite for my own good," I told Mr. Amos the next morning.

He drew a card from the deck between us. "Not so's I've noticed," he said, and discarded.

"Then why are we moving?" I drew a card. "I didn't have a thing to say about it. Not one thing! Why do grown-ups act like you've got a voice in the decision when they know darn well you don't and they'll do whatever they please?"

I tried to concentrate on finding a good discard, but my heart wasn't in it. Mr. Amos chewed his toothpick vigorously and impatiently, warning me that I was slowing down the game.

Finally I shocked him by just throwing all my cards onto the step.

"Say now, say now," he said in a soothing way. "On the television set it says Branson, Missouri, is exploding, music-wise. It says one could compare Branson, Missouri, to Nashville, Tennessee. So now, I guess it could be instead of a small fish in a small pond, Burl has a chance to be a small fish in a big pond. Or somesuch thing like that. How's that go?"

"Big fish in a small pond," I muttered. I rolled my eyes and buried my chin farther in my hands. It was hard to imagine 200-pound Burl as a fish of any kind.

"Besides, girl," Mr. Amos continued, picking up the cards slowly, one at a time, making a careful, organized job of it, "it ain't like you have that much to leave behind you here that I can see. Your mama wastes her pretty, smart self by waitressing up to the Winstead's. And you—well, if you had all that many friends, you wouldn't be setting here on the concrete stairsteps, playing rummy with a old janitor on a pretty August day, now would you?"

My chest was tightening up. "I can't help it if kids here are snooty," I told him. "Next month in seventh grade they'll probably be even snootier."

"So," said Mr. Amos, "hear what I say, then?"

I took a deep breath and blew it out.

"Mr. Amos, there's something about Burl that I just don't trust," I confided in a whisper. *"Especially* since he asked me about hair transplants."

I shouldn't have whispered. Mr. Amos is getting pretty deaf, and he evidently didn't hear me.

"Listen, Elizy, what I think is that you prefer even the snooty kids here to the kids you have to up and meet for the first time there. You figure you won't have a plan for hiding from them like you have a plan here. But girl, you

11

don't have to hide. You can up and be anybody you want in a brand new place! Anybody!"

Mr. Amos had never talked to me in exactly that way before. I had to admit it was something to think about.

"If you could do that, be anybody, who would you be?" I asked him.

"A reader," he answered right away. "A man with a roomful of *National Geographic*s and the ability to comprehend the words and not just guess the story by studying the pictures."

"Well, I'd be rich," I said. "Rich enough to not worry about anything. I'd have wonderful hair and perfect clothes and everybody would want to be exactly like me because I'd be so cool."

"Sounds like Burl's big plan in life," Mr. Amos said, then snorted out a little laugh. "Heh, heh."

♦ ♦ ♦

We packed fast, since Mama wanted to avoid having to pay another month's rent. By the end of the week our stuff was boxed up and loaded onto the back of Burl's truck.

Mr. Amos was basically the only person I had to say good-bye to.

"You be remembering what I told you?" he whispered to me as we stood there on the sidewalk watching Mama and Burl ease themselves into the cab of the truck. It was already crowded with odds and ends, Mama's houseplants and stuff. "About not being afraid to just up and be whoever you want to be in this here new place? This could be a real adventure for you, Elizy."

I squinted at him. "I guess," I said.

He nodded, then gave my shoulder a good-bye squeeze and turned and began his slow climb up the stone stairs, back into the building.

I slid into the frayed seat beside Mama. I couldn't call out a good-bye because I had a lump in my throat, but I waved to Mr. Amos's back, and somehow he knew and raised his arm to wave to me.

◆ ◆ ◆

In an hour we were out of the suburbs and in the open country, and the flat land I was used to seeing started buckling up and becoming less predictable, like someone had kicked it around. Things got greener and greener and hillier and hillier as we went south.

The countryside was pretty, and most of the towns we drove through were neat and orderly and made you think the people in them must be organized and friendly and happy. But here and there were ugly little towns stuck like warts into the hillsides, filled with rusty car graveyards, and shacks.

"Is this Gouge Eye a pretty town?" I asked Burl a few times.

The third or fourth time he decided to answer. He pushed his hat back a little and frowned at the road ahead of us. "Well, Eliza, maybe *pretty*'s not the word I'd use," he said. "Maybe you'd more like call Gouge Eye, well . . . how about 'broken in.' Broken in, like a good old scuffed boot that don't no longer hurt your toes hardly a bit."

I was speechless, and just stared out the window again as the fields spilled by me.

And then, finally, we turned off the highway onto a gravel road and went up and down a couple of steep hills, then crossed a rickety bridge with a sign beside it— TWISTED CREEK, LOAD LIMIT 10 TONS.

"Just ahead now, ladies," Burl said, and Mama giggled and moved even closer to Burl. She took his hand and put his arm around her shoulders.

A clump of dusty trees was coming up ahead of us. As we got nearer, they thinned and I saw a skinny gray cat scratching itself on the pole of a green sign that had several bullet holes in it. The sign read GOUGE EYE, MISSOURI, POPULATION 435.

Just beyond the sign, two huge, round, silver towers shot like bloated spaceships into the sky. One of them had black letters spelling MISSOURI FARM ASSOCIATION GRAIN ELEVATOR running around it, and the other had a big red flashing light on top, which was cracked in a couple of places. A smashed-looking flat gray building huddled beneath one of the towers, with a stained cardboard sign in its window reading MFA FEED STORE.

"Notice the cats," Burl said. "They stay by the dozen up close around the elevator and feed store, catching rats." He smiled, obviously hoping to impress me since I love cats. But Mama grimaced.

Bad move, Burl, I thought, and felt a little jolt of satisfaction. He should have known she'd hate the thought of all those rats.

A bunch of trucks were parked around a gas station with two soda machines and a newspaper machine outside, and several more trucks nudged up close to what looked like a restaurant next door. The plate glass window running across the front of the restaurant had green lettering—SKEETER'S FINE FOOD AND DRINK. Smaller green letters beneath that warned—*no shoes, no shirt, no service.* Someone had taped a sheet of notebook paper just under those letters and had written on it "this means you, Jay Roy!"

Across from the elevator, gas station, and restaurant was a big skating rink–sized metal barn of a building with HECKLEMAN'S LUMBERTERIA across the door. Waist-high weeds grew all around the building and twisted through a bunch of strange, round, orange metal things stacked four or five deep in front of it. A few old boards were soaking in a mud puddle by a For Sale sign.

"Heckleman's has closed," Burl said sadly. "With money tight the farmers don't buy so much to build with these days. They mostly make do with what they already got. Say, they might tear down an old chicken house and use that wood for part of a barn."

"What are those . . . big orange things?" I asked.

"Pig feeders," Burl answered. "Anybody what wants to buy one can find old Randy Heckleman at the bar and get him to load them up one, I guess." Mama looked quickly at Burl. "Not to say Skeeter's is a bar!" he added. "No, no, Skeeter's is a perfectly respectable family cafe. A real nice place to work at, too, I'd say."

Something about the way he said that made me wonder uneasily—was part of the plan that Mama would get a job at that place, that Skeeter's?

The truck hit a pothole and we all three bounced. "Whoa!" Burl said, and Mama laughed.

Next to Skeeter's Fine Food and Drink was a brick building that had been painted bright turquoise. A woman worked outside, taping some handmade signs to the windows. "You bet we're open Sundays!" one said. "You bet our WORMS are FRESH!" said another. There were a couple of decorations on the signs—little drawings of worms I guessed, though they looked more like intestines. The loose skin under the woman's arms flapped like flags as she worked. A tiny girl was smashed up against the woman's large hip, sucking her thumb and wrapping her hair around one wrist.

"That's Isabelle Ferguson and her little Janelle," Burl said, waving out the window. The woman saw and waved exuberantly back. "Isabelle has a bait shop there and lives upstairs of it."

I saw her store sign, then, propped against a chunk of concrete out front—ISABELLE'S BAIT SHOPPE.

"What are those buildings across the street?" Mama asked, and I thought I heard something a little dulled down slip into the bright, super-cheerful voice she'd been using all day. "Is that the business district?"

Where she was looking, four brick buildings sagged together like tired friends.

"Well, I tell you what, it used to be," Burl said. "That

16

big building on the corner used to be the bank, but it closed about three years back. B.J. Turley bought the building and started an auction house and poultry business there. Folks come from all over to bid on the junk he auctions every Saturday night, and to buy eggs. He brings eggs in from his farm and stores them during the week in the old bank safe. Uh, the two buildings next to it have been vacant for years and years."

"But there's a grocery store!" she said, pointing to where the fourth brick building wore a bright orange TUCKER'S GROCERY sign like a silly hat above its big windows.

"And again I say, it used to be it was a store," Burl said softly, sounding worried as Mama ducked from under his arm and moved to sit a smidgeon closer to me. "The grocery closed just fairly recently, in fact. Jimmy Muller, the owner, retired, see, and him and his uncle Bob decided to buy them a cabin down in . . ."

"Burl!" Mama jerked her pretty head toward him so fast her red curls moved like lightning through the cab of the truck. "I really don't care about Jimmy Muller's uncle Bob's plans. I care about living in a place without . . . without a single . . ."

She buried her face in her hands and began shaking her head.

"Without a single store?" Burl guessed timidly.

"Sign of life?" I added. "Redeeming quality?"

Mama took her hands from her face and stared at me with a look that made my stomach sink. It made me

17

remember her face in the kitchen the night Burl came back—*Eliza, I am so tired.*

"Just kidding!" I told her, smiling cheerfully and even forcing a laugh. After a few seconds Burl laughed along. Mama looked at him, then looked again at me, and I pushed my smile wider and wider until she finally shrugged, shook her head, and smiled weakly back at me.

CHAPTER
—3—

We drove on two more blocks, past about a dozen little houses. Two of them were bright banana yellow and one of the others was decorated with metal things, such as old license plates. None of the houses here seemed exactly planned, but appeared to have accidentally sprouted from the yards like the dandelions that inhabited each crack in the sidewalk.

We passed a slender white church surrounded by a black iron fence and set far off the messy street. The churchyard was mowed so short it looked shaved, and none of the shaggy weeds from the yards on either side had been allowed in.

"Gettin' close!" Burl said.

We started down another block. On the corner was a vacant lot, which gave a clear view of the fields beyond the town. At the far edge of those fields I could see the woods surrounding the creek we'd crossed before we reached town, Twisted Creek.

"Hey, somebody's walking out there!" I yelled, surprised by the sight of a person trudging alone through a patch of knee-high fuzzy weeds. At first I thought it was a boy, but then I decided it might be a girl, tall and skinny with short and spiky yellow hair. She was going toward the woods, and I could have sworn she was carrying a book in one hand and an ax in the other. I thrust my head out the window, trying to catch another look, and yelled back over my shoulder to Burl and Mama. "Hey, you guys! There's a weird kid out there in those gross weeds, and she's got an ax!"

"Soybeans, Eliza. That's not weeds, it's soybeans," Burl mumbled. Then they both just ignored me. They were leaning forward, and Burl was pointing down the block and across the street.

"Okay, now, this here is the home of our nearest neighbors." He pointed to a little green shoebox of a house which was surrounded by stacks and stacks of wood. A For Sale sign like the one at the lumberyard hung, rusty, from a black frame in the front yard.

"And . . . there she is! There's our place!"

He pulled the truck to the curb in front of a pink trailer.

It wasn't big or little. It wasn't fancy or shacky. There wasn't all that much you could say about it except that it was pink. Not dark pink, not light pink. Just pink.

"Well!" said Mama, biting her bottom lip, her eyes just a little too bright. "What a pretty color. Right, Eliza? Now, let's see, just what exactly would you call that color?"

"Pink," I replied.

♦ ♦ ♦

We got busy unloading the truck and moving things in. There was a room for me tucked into one back corner of the trailer, and it seemed so much like a little cabin in a boat that to my surprise I liked it immediately. You could sit on the bed and reach everything you might want—the dresser, the little desk, the closet. I felt almost like a turtle, with my room wrapped close and cozy around me.

When I had my stuff put away I went outside and sat on one of the three wooden steps that led up to the trailer's front door. Mama and Burl were reorganizing the kitchen, laughing, and clattering things around. They had the radio turned up high. It was dark by then, and the fireflies seemed to wink in time to the country western songs pouring out the kitchen windows.

Sitting on the steps like that reminded me of Mr. Amos, and I hugged my knees up under my chin and thought about that advice he'd given me, to be anybody I wanted to be in this new place. Actually I'd thought a lot about it already the past few days, since he'd first mentioned it, and I just couldn't get past the fact that what I really wanted to be was like the rich kids, with their salon haircuts and their designer jeans. Those were the really cool kids. They did most of the whispering behind people's backs, but nobody had the nerve to whisper about them.

The guys my mother had dated all year had been men she'd met at Winstead's. They were the kind of men you could easily picture ordering a hamburger and a malt, though my mother looked like Julia Roberts and should have been with men who jetted around the world and had gobs of credit cards and gave her diamonds. If for just one day she could have been like Cinderella, in the right elegant place, all dressed up fancy and looking rich, I knew for sure somebody cool would have snapped her up in a second.

Instead she got Burl.

It would be kind of like that at this new school. If I could just somehow make a cool first impression I might get snapped up by the cool, popular kids before they learned I wasn't even a bit semirich. But I'd tried to figure out how to make a cool first impression about a thousand times the past few days. The problem was that cool people didn't act like they were trying. I mean, you could spot somebody that was trying to be cool, and you didn't think they were cool *at all*.

I sighed and bounced my chin on my knees and leaned forward to look down the block. Everything was dark except for the red light on top of the elevator, blinking, and the big rectangular window at Skeeter's bar, or cafe, or whatever it was.

I held my breath and listened. The darkness was a much quieter darkness than in Kansas City. The quiet was so thick it felt like it was a living thing, wrapping fuzzy arms around you.

Shivering, I jumped up and walked into the yard, kicking my feet through the scraggly grass to make a little comforting squish of noise.

As I got closer to the little green shoebox house next door, I began to hear a snarl of noise, which got louder with each step I took. At first I thought the people in that house had their TV turned up really loud, but then I realized I was hearing real, live people. A man was yelling, and a woman was crying in a truly miserable, beat-down way. I felt embarrassed listening, but walked a little closer anyway. There was also some crashing noise, like things were being thrown around.

I was pretty shocked. I'd never heard even television people carry on quite like those people were carrying on.

Our trailer door opened and I ran full-speed back through the yard to the trailer steps, feeling as guilty as if I'd been spying.

"You okay out here?" Mama asked. She was framed in the doorway and her slim shape cut a dark cookie-cutter hole from the brightness inside the trailer. "Hey now, baby, can you believe it?" She held the sides of the doorway with both hands and bent into the darkness to whisper down to me so Burl wouldn't hear. "Here we are in a town without a single store?"

"Well, there's a bait shop," I reminded her, and we both had a laugh before she went inside and shut the door.

I hurried back out into the yard and eagerly listened again. The awful argument next door was still going on.

Then something moved across the street, and I hit the ground, lying on my stomach and spying through the tall grass.

It was the weird, spiky-haired girl I'd seen earlier. The

23

lights of a passing car glinted off the blade of her ax as she emerged from the vacant lot on the corner, crossed the street, and entered the yard of the green shoebox house next door. She jumped the For Sale sign without really looking at it, but stopped a few yards from the front porch.

Something big-sounding hit a wall inside the house and shattered, and the woman whimpered. The girl with the ax and the fat book crouched quickly down in the shadows the woodpiles made.

There was a quiet lull for a few seconds, and the cowboy on Burl's radio far behind me sang out, "It ain't easy lovin' you!"

Then there was another crash next door, and the front door of the green house banged open. The girl, still crouching low, skittered deeper into the shadows as a man stormed out, jumped the front steps, and got into the pickup truck parked behind Burl's pickup on the street. He slammed the door of the truck, and seconds later squealed away from the curb.

I didn't want to embarrass the girl by letting her know I'd seen anything just now. On the other hand, I was dying to get a closer look at her. I squinted hard, trying to see through the deep shadows.

The front door of the house opened again, just a little and slowly this time. I could see the dim outline of a woman just inside the house, holding the door partly open like a shield in front of her.

"Dierdre? Dierdre, you out there?" the woman whisper-called.

The girl in the shadows didn't answer. The woman called again, then went back inside. When she'd closed the door, the girl jumped up and ran out of the yard and back across the street. She disappeared back the way she'd come, into the empty lot on the corner that was the entrance to the soybean field and the woods beyond.

I was almost positive her hands were empty now. I waited a few seconds to be sure the woman wouldn't come back out of the house, then I got up and ran, bush to bush, through the edge of our yard and into theirs. When I reached the woodpiles that circled her yard like a belt, I crouched and walked duck-style through the shadows.

The ax was easy to see, glowing there on the ground. I had to feel around before I found the book, though, and then I had to sneak, still crouching, out of the shadows and closer to the house to make out the title.

"The Adventures of Huckleberry Finn," I read in a whisper.

It was a fat book. A very fat book, with small print and a Pertle Creek Public Library sticker on the inside of the cover.

"Don't it make my brown eyes blue?" whined the woman on Burl's radio. I turned back toward the trailer. At this distance it looked exactly like a bubble gum cigar. You could see Mama's and Burl's shadows against the kitchen curtains, slow dancing to the music.

I turned away from them, toward the vacant lot on the corner across the street. The waving weeds over there beckoned me like fingers.

Mr. Amos had said to think of this as an adventure.

I tossed the fat book back into the shadows and ran across the street and into the night, following the spiky-haired girl.

♦ ♦ ♦

About halfway through the vacant lot the dim light from the houses and from Skeeter's trickled away to darkness. Bugs began buzzing and dive-bombing right past my ears, acting way braver than they acted in the daytime, or in the city at any time.

"Hey!" I called out. The soybean field started where the lot left off, and loomed ahead like a black ocean with the woods rising in the distance like a tidal wave.

Nobody answered my call, so I ran faster, concentrating on the pumping of my legs so I wouldn't think of anything else. Cockleburrs caught at my ankles like tiny teeth.

Finally, my ears ringing and my chest sore, I reached the edge of the woods.

"Hey, say something!" I called into the trees, then stopped to bend, and puff in some air. I straightened, and put my hands around my mouth like a megaphone. "You in there or what?"

Suddenly, strange humanoid whooping sounds came pouring from the woods. While I stood too paralyzed with fear to think of anything but how mad I was at Mr.

Amos for getting me into this mess, something came lurching out of the darkness, right at my hip level, and slugged me in the side.

"Tagged! Beat you back to base!" it screeched, shining a light in my eyes like aliens do when they're getting ready to drag you to their spaceship.

Another shadow separated from the black hole that was the woods. I could tell from the loose, slow, and bony way it moved it had to be either a second space alien, a walking skeleton, or the spiky-haired girl.

"Jay Roy, don't be such a wienie," the shadow mumbled. "That's the new kid Burl brought here. She's not even playing yet, and you know it."

CHAPTER
—◦4◦—

R ight then the top of the full moon poked up above the
dark fringe of trees, making everything much brighter.
The spooky, shadowy things that were emerging from the
edge of the woods turned into kids and two or three
frowsy, loose-tongued dogs. The spiky-haired girl stood
silently watching me as the other kids moved forward and
fell in behind her. Her arms were crossed and her feet
were planted far apart like she was Peter Pan and the other
kids were the Lost Boys.

Something soft slipped into my hand. I jumped and
looked down to see the little bait shop girl Burl had called
Janelle, leaning against my leg with her thumb in her
mouth.

"See? She's playing now!" Jay Roy screamed, shining
that obnoxious flashlight into my eyes again.

Just then wavy voices from back in town came floating
across the soybean field.

"The mothers are calling," the spiky-haired girl said,
and I noticed her voice was lower and flatter than practi-

cally any girl's voice I'd ever heard before. "Go on home, you guys."

Janelle dropped my hand and ran into the field, and the other kids followed, like giant moths going toward their own lights.

The spiky-haired, Peter Pan girl didn't move, though. I remembered her name, then—the name that woman, evidently her mother, had called her—Dierdre.

An eerie howling sound started up in the woods.

"Coyotes, but they're so deep in Hilley's Woods there aren't even paths back that far," the girl, Dierdre, said. "They're just confused. They think the mothers' voices are other coyotes calling them. Every night all summer we play hide and seek with a flashlight in the woods, and every night they howl like that. Don't be afraid."

"Are you kidding? I'm not afraid," I immediately told her, like someone cool would have done.

She put her hands in the pockets of her cutoff jeans and took a couple of steps toward me. "Tomorrow night you'll have to be 'it' first or Jay Roy will pout around and make our lives miserable."

I was close enough to see her clearly for the first time. One foot was forward and her opposite hip was cocked so her knee on that side could jiggle—the only sign that possibly she was slightly nervous about meeting me, a stranger. Then I noticed a second sign—she was sucking in her left cheek. She was several inches taller than me and her sweat-spiked short yellow hair looked a little like that crown thing the Statue of Liberty wears.

29

"I might not even be here tomorrow night," I informed her. "I'm just visiting. My mother and I live in Kansas City."

"Before he left to get you, Burl said you and your mother were moving in with him," she said matter-of-factly. "He told everybody you had dead-ended up there in the city by yourselves. He says you two have been begging him and begging him to bring you here because you need a big strong man like him to take care of you. He says your mother is pretty but scatter-brained, and her lucky day was the day he danced right into her life and swept her off her feet. He says that with a little time he may just even be able to straighten out your attitude problem. He says . . ."

My mouth dropped open. In fact, I felt like somebody had cranked it open and was pouring gallons of hot liquid into me.

"That's not true!" I yelled. "Every word of that is absolutely, stupidly, disgustingly false!"

"Oh," she said, like that settled it.

Then her eyes flickered, and she frowned at something over my shoulder and in the distance. "I've got to go," she mumbled. "My dad just got home."

She began running through the soybeans. I turned to watch her and saw the lights go off on a tiny truck parked on a tiny street in front of a tiny house next to a tiny trailer; all of this inside a tiny, ugly town the other side of the deep fields from us.

Why should I even go back there, where Mama and I

30

were just things braggadocious old Burl could pretend to take care of? I *knew* we shouldn't trust Burl! It would just serve them right if I stayed out here and made them sick with worry—when they could pull their goo-goo eyes off each other long enough to even notice I was gone, that is.

The girl stopped and turned back to me. "You coming?"

"For all some stupid people care we should just stay out here till we rot," I answered, hoping my voice wasn't quivering.

"Yeah," she agreed. "So, you coming?"

◆ ◆ ◆

We ran together back across the field. I easily slipped inside the trailer and tiptoed past where Mama and Burl cuddled together on the sofa, dozing and watching some gross old movie about gangsters.

" 'Night, darlin'," Mama called groggily as I went down the hall. "Sleep tight."

Her words caught me just as I was passing Burl's bedroom, where I noticed he had his many pairs of boots set up like a little parade along one of the walls. Why couldn't he just follow that boot parade, right out the door and out of our lives?

I lay awake for a long time in my turtle-shell room thinking about what a creep Burl was—that liar. There was no way anybody could be a cool, new person in a place where somebody had beat them to the punch and made them sound like a jerk with another jerk for a mother. The second I could get Mama alone I'd tell her what he'd said and we'd be on our way back to K.C. so fast it would make his old bald head spin.

◆ ◆ ◆

When it was just barely light outside, a thousand dentists' drills all came on at once somewhere near my ear. I tried to jump out of bed, but there wasn't enough floor space and I cracked my knee on the wall. I fell back on the mattress, groaning, just as Dierdre's face pressed itself into the loose screen of my window.

"You're in there," she informed me. "So come on out."

"Dierdre!" Half asleep, disoriented, I stood up on the mattress and bent to look down at her, then dropped down, and immediately clutched my sore knee again. "What's happening out there? What's going on?"

"What?" she said, shrugging. Then, "Oh, you mean the noise? Dad's cutting wood like he does every morning he's sober enough. That's his chain saw."

I flopped onto my back and covered myself, face and all, with my sheet. "Get me out of here!" I moaned, kicking my feet.

There was silence for about a minute, but I could tell by the way the weak, early morning sunlight was blocked that Dierdre was still in the window. I finally took the sheet down as far as my eyes. Sure enough, she was still there. Now she had one arm up, shielding her eyes so she could see me better, and in the hand attached to that arm she held her ax.

"Okay," she said, and shrugged. "I'll try."

"Try what?"

"Try to get you out," she said matter-of-factly, and left.

I lay there puzzled for about five seconds, then I had an awful thought and leapt out of my bed and into the hall-way. As I ran limping past the open doorway of Burl's messy, boot-lined room, I pictured Dierdre hacking down our front door with her ax.

Mama and Burl were sitting at the little table in the combination kitchen-living room of the trailer, holding hands.

"Stop her! She may be crazy!" I yelled to them.

"Who's crazy, hon?" Mama asked, smiling at me over the rim of her coffee mug. Her hair was messy and tangled but still pretty in a wild way, and her skin was pinkish and beautiful.

"I am, cuddle bug," Burl whispered huskily, as he leaned farther across the table, getting toast crumbs smashed into the stomach of his shirt, and grinned into Mama's face. "This here cowboy's crazy in love with you, woman."

There was no time to throw up—I had to keep Dierdre from destroying the trailer.

"The girl next door has an ax!" I yelled. "Hide!"

"Okay, honey, whatever you say," Mama murmured, but they both just sat there wrinkling their noses at each other, not even listening to me.

I limped past them and crouched by the three big windows that lined the edge of the trailer where the TV was, the windows that gave you a view in three directions.

I carefully peered out the window on my right, expecting to see Dierdre balanced on one of our three wooden steps, ready to take a swing at our front door.

But instead I saw her out the big middle window. She was calmly walking up the steps of her own porch. She stopped to balance the ax against the porch swing, then she went inside.

I turned around and slid down to sit cross-legged on the floor, rubbing my knee. I couldn't bring myself to look in the kitchen, toward Burl, that liar. But the conversation he and Mama were having began to sink into my brain.

". . . guess I should go on over there to the restaurant and at least introduce myself today, then. You think so, Burl?"

"Well, hon, I do think that would be the thing to do, yes. I mean, I'll be gone long days at a time, gigging with the band, and this'll give you something to occupy you. And besides, every nickel helps with the band doing so good. Fame don't come cheap."

"Go on over where?" I asked. "Introduce yourself to who?"

The phone rang and Mama went into the hall to get it. I sat glaring at Burl while she was gone, but he just crammed scrambled eggs into his mouth and didn't notice.

"Oh, the sweetest thing!" Mama said, coming back into the kitchen with her hands squeezed happily together. "The sweet woman next door, Hannah her name is, just invited Eliza to go to the Pertle Creek public swimming pool with her daughter, Diedre."

"Dierdre," I mumbled, correcting her pronunciation. "Dierdre, with an 'r' in each syllable. She's the kid I keep trying to tell you may be an ax murderer."

"Well, Hannah said they'll leave in twenty minutes, so you'd better hustle and see if you can find a swimsuit, honey. Maybe that red one I picked up at that garage sale last spring will fit you by now, you think?"

I opened my mouth, thinking I had a right to at least register some kind of opinion about this swimming plan. But just then Burl turned to face me head-on for the first time that morning, and the shock drove everything else from my mind.

Sticking out from under his hat was a clot of orange fluffy stuff that looked to be made of spun sugar, like that cotton candy they have at carnivals.

"Burl, you bought yourself a toupee!" I squawked.

"Yes, and isn't it attractive, too," Mama said, chewing one thumbnail doubtfully.

CHAPTER
—5—

I wore the red two-piece suit Mama had found at that garage sale to the pool that day, and Dierdre wore this flowered one-piece that looked about twelve sizes too big for her, probably also from somebody's garage sale. My suit was cut too high at the waist to be exactly called a bikini, though I tried to push it down to belly-button level every time I remembered.

Dierdre's mother, Hannah, drove us to the pool in the same pickup Dierdre's father had peeled away from the curb the night before. Every time she touched the brake several empty beer cans came rolling out from under the seat, and Dierdre swatted them back under with her heels.

"My, my, I can't tell you, Eliza, how wonderful it is having you and your mother move in next door," Hannah said when we were less than a block from home, going by the prim white church. Mama had guessed about right—Dierdre's mother was definitely what you'd call "sweet," and talked in the kind of quiet, hesitant voice that told you she would never hurt a living thing. "I've been just craving and craving another woman to talk with, and I was afraid to death that Dierdre would have to start junior high alone."

So this Dierdre was my age and going into seventh grade. My eyes darted sideways to her, where she sat between her mother and me with her knees bent, grasshopperlike, nearly to her chin because her long feet were up on the hump thing in the middle of the floor of the truck.

"None of those kids from last night are our age?" I asked.

"We're the oldest kids in Gouge Eye," Dierdre responded.

I looked back out the bug-splattered windshield and tried to think of something polite to say to Dierdre's mother. I knew that once I had a chance to tell Mama about Burl's lies we wouldn't be staying here long, but somehow that didn't seem like a good topic of conversation.

"It should be fun going to school in Branson," I said, playing along to be polite. "Exciting, I mean."

Dierdre turned her head to frown at me, and Hannah said, "Branson?"

"We get bused to the junior high in Pertle Creek," Dierdre said. "It's six miles closer than Branson, in the opposite direction."

I tried not to act shocked. After all, I told myself, it won't matter—you'll be back in Kansas City by then.

I shrugged. "Whatever," I said.

We putt-putted past the bait shop and Skeeter's and the elevator and feed store, all the time dodging dogs who were lying asleep in the street and had no apparent desire to move out of our way. We went past the "Gouge Eye, Missouri, population 435" sign and turned onto the highway.

The truck had barely picked up enough speed to shift through all four gears when Hannah suddenly slammed on the brakes and we fishtailed to a stop in the middle of the road. She shoved the gearshift into neutral, stomped down on the emergency brake, and got out of the truck, leaving us to idle there in the middle of the highway.

"Don't worry. Nobody's going to come," Dierdre told me, as if she could possibly know.

Hannah trotted along in front of the truck, and bent down to pick up a turtle that had been snoozing near the center line of the highway. She twisted around like a short, pudgy discus-hurler, then untwisted and let that turtle fly, into the high weeds beside the road. Then she trotted back, got in the truck, and put it into gear, smiling.

"Mama's goal is to save all animals," Dierdre explained.

Hannah shrugged like someone who has been given a huge compliment but is trying to be modest about it. "Actually, I would have dearly loved to be a veterinarian. But of course, life has a way of curving around on you."

"Throwing you a curve," Dierdre corrected.

"Why, yes!" her mother said, and laughed.

♦ ♦ ♦

Pertle Creek turned out to be a town of 2,887 people, according to the green sign at the city limits. The public swimming pool was in the center of a hilly park filled with swing sets and white-painted picnic tables. Along one side of the park ran a wide river with fishermen in lawn chairs lining it.

"Well, gals, I'll go do a little grocery shopping and such, and I'll pick you up in a couple of hours, okey dokey?" Hannah said, as she let us out by the admission window.

Dierdre got in line and I got in line behind her. I squinted through the chain-link fence surrounding the pool and spotted several groups of kids who seemed to be about our age and would probably be going to Pertle Creek Junior High. Their suits were mostly in hot, neon colors, and most of them had tans and swingy-looking hair, lots shorter than mine, but longer and a zillion times more stylish, even wet, than Dierdre's.

Dierdre turned to me. "Why did Burl say you have an attitude problem?" she asked, right out of the blue.

I think my mouth dropped open and I shook my head in disbelief. "How in the world should I know? I can't believe you'd even ask a person a question like that!"

She turned back around, and a minute later we reached the front of the line, paid for our tickets, and Dierdre got a metal basket. In the dressing room we crammed our shoes and the T-shirts we'd brought into it.

"I just thought maybe you did something. Got arrested or something," she said, straightening up and looking at me in the big mirror that was spread along one wall.

She was long and whitish and bony, and her wild suit hung on her like a wilting bouquet. I was shorter and slightly less white, but in the glaring light I could see pinkish fade lines in my red suit.

"For your information, I never had the slightest bit of trouble in the city," I told her. My jaws were aching real bad, like when you suck a sour candy. "I had lots of good friends and they never had the slightest bit of trouble either."

I grabbed at my flat dark hair, trying to work it into a braid or something. That glaring light also showed up the horrible black hairs I'd always had all over my arms from wrists to shoulders, growing from them like wires.

"Still," she said in that flat, low voice of hers, "it's funny he'd say that particular thing."

"Dierdre, will you please just drop it?" I hissed in a whisper. "Just drop it, okay?"

I shoved past her and stomped out into the noisy glare of the pool area. Right outside the dressing room was the diving board edge of the pool, and behind the diving boards three girls were sprawled, slick and shiny-looking, propped on their elbows on bright towels. There were cute boys with them—horsing around and laughing. A couple of the boys had radios with headphones. They all had sodas and chips, too, partway hidden under their towels since a big sign in the dressing room had warned that food and drinks weren't supposed to be brought into the pool area.

I moved quickly on so those popular kids wouldn't think I was gawking at them. As I moved along the edge of the pool I passed several other groups about our age, splashing and pulling each other off the sides and under the water, diving for pennies, racing, and stuff like that.

"Do you know any of these guys?" I asked Dierdre when she finally came out and caught up to me. "I mean, where do you want to spread our towels?"

Just then a squeal came from over near the kiddie pool, exactly as far from the diving boards as you could get.

"Deeeee-errr-dra! Deer-drah-Deer-drah! Come here! C'mere-c'mere-c'mere! Dierdre! Come here by me!"

I squinted toward the sound and saw a short girl in a brown one-piece with an old-fashioned little skirt at the bottom, which didn't begin to hide the doughy tops of her white thighs. She was wearing little diving goggles which were so covered with drips she couldn't possibly have seen through them. She was jumping up and down in the kiddie pool, splattering water into the eyes of a couple of astonished-looking toddlers.

"I know that girl. That's Nancy Petrinsen. I see her in the public library sometimes," Dierdre said, waving and heading us toward the kiddie pool.

"Is . . . is she the only person here you know?" I asked, but Dierdre was already walking in that loose and boylike way of hers toward the kiddie pool.

The walk to the kiddie pool seemed endless. I kept my

41

eyes straight ahead and stared at Dierdre's chalky, callused heels, wishing this humiliating afternoon was over.

◆ ◆ ◆

"So, what's her name?" Nancy asked Dierdre as we spread our towels by the kiddie-pool fence. "She your cousin or something?"

"My name is Eliza Marie Branniman," I said, flopping down on my stomach and turning my head away from them. "And no, for your information, I'm not Dierdre's cousin. As it happens, I'm just visiting next door to her. I'm from Kansas City, as it happens."

"What's that 'as it happens' stuff?" Nancy whispered to Dierdre. "Is that how they talk in the city or something?"

Dierdre must have made some gesture in answer, but my back was to them so I don't know what it was.

"I just adore your suit, Dierdre," Nancy said then. "Is hers supposed to have those little pink streaks in it or something?"

I sat up. "Yes!" I answered.

I slid quickly into the shallow kiddie pool and lay on the bottom for a minute, hoping the water would even up the color of my suit. Sounds above the surface seemed far away and soothing, except for Nancy's voice, which was nasal and droning enough to set it apart.

When I came to the surface I stayed most of the way in the water, looking around. I soon noticed that practically no girls our age were actually swimming. Only the boys were getting into the water much, and the girls were all lounging close to the edge, working on tans, talking, kicking at the boys when they splashed or grabbed their ankles.

"Let's move our towels to over beside the adult pool," I suggested, but you'd have thought from the way Nancy acted that I'd suggested moving permanently to Saturn.

"Why would we want to go over there?" she demanded, looking at a couple of the splashing boys and cringing. "All those people are just so . . . juvenile!"

Dierdre didn't say anything. She just slid into the kiddie pool and started doing laps in the three-foot-deep water.

So the rest of the afternoon I stayed there with them, but I certainly didn't swim. I just lounged, working on a tan, until finally about a hundred years later Dierdre's mother showed up to take us back to Gouge Eye.

CHAPTER
~6~

You girls can't guess what just happened!" Hannah
squealed the second Dierdre and I got back into the truck
that afternoon. She had her hands made into fists and kept
bouncing them happily against the steering wheel. "Just
guess! I bet you can't! No, you never will be able to in a
million years!"

She gave the steering wheel another excited little drum-
roll, then, finally using her hands like a normal person,
started backing out of the parking lot.

"Give us a hint," Dierdre suggested.

"Well, it was something good," Hannah said, but of
course that was so obvious it really wasn't much of a
hint.

"Involving . . . money?" Dierdre asked, and I thought
I heard her low, flat voice waver a little on the word
"money."

"Yes!" Hannah exclaimed, laughing. "Yes, yes, yes!"

We were out on the road leading back to Gouge Eye
by then, and the truck lurched four quick times as Han-

nah accidentally pumped the gas pedal with each "yes."

"Five-hun-dred-dollars," Hannah whispered, then drew in a deep breath and let it out. "Can you imagine, girls? You buy one little lottery ticket, the 'Scratch-3' game where if you scratch off three matching numbers you win that amount, and you're standing there thinking you shouldn't be wasting an entire dollar, and then you scratch and see one five hundred, then scratch another place and see another five hundred, and then you're thinking 'well, this is fine but there's no chance that lightning will strike in this third box,' but you scratch and see another five, then another zero, then a third zero, and then you just start screaming and screaming and jumping all around and the other customers start slapping you on the back, congratulating you, and one lady standing right behind you in the grocery line even gives you a bunch of her bananas like you'd give Miss America roses!"

As Hannah talked, I noticed a change in Dierdre, or at least in Dierdre's back, which was all I could see of her since she was turning more eagerly toward her mother all the time. I hadn't noticed before that her shoulders were slightly stooped, but I saw them getting straighter. When Hannah stopped for breath, Dierdre was turned completely sideways toward her, and her knobby shoulders were so high her shoulder blades seemed like sharp wings.

"So we won five hundred dollars, free and clear?" Dierdre asked in a rush. "How fast can we get our hands on it, in time for Dad to . . ."

"Oh, Dierdre!" Hannah raised one hand to her mouth.

"Oh, honey, I didn't win that money. The lady in front of me in the grocery line did. Honey, I was the lady who gave her the bananas."

Dierdre slumped back in her seat and stared out the windshield, expressionless. Neither she nor her mother said another word the rest of the way home, and to tell the truth I was too exhausted by the nerve-wracking afternoon to try to think up anything to say either.

◆ ◆ ◆

I perked up, though, when I saw that Burl's truck was gone from in front of the trailer. I was more anxious than ever to talk in private to Mama, to give her the scoop on the real Burl so we could pack up and leave.

But when I burst in, Mama's purse was open on the kitchen table, and Mama herself was scrunched down, leaning with her elbows on the counter, using the smudged but shiny side of the toaster as a mirror while she put on lipstick. She had on a saggy light green dress cinched at the waist by a tongue-shaped white apron. Something glittered along the bottom of her skirt, at knee level.

"Hi, sweetie! Guess what!" She whirled toward me and I saw the name "Juanita" embroidered in red cursive across one chest pocket of that huge, shapeless dress. Her eyes were bright like they got when she was excited or nervous. "I got a new job! At Skeeter's Cafe! Right here in town! Isn't that great?"

She tucked her lipstick back into her purse, dusted the toast crumbs off her elbows, and held her arms out, open for a hug. But I took a step backward. "You look like Cinderella," I told her.

She seemed confused. "You mean you think I look like I'm going to a big old fancy ball?" She laughed, looking down at the sacklike skirt of her new uniform, pulling at the sides. "Well, thank you, but to tell the truth, the last waitress, Juanita, was several sizes bigger than me, and I really feel like I swim in this thing. It is nice and starchy, though, I'll have to admit. I didn't have time to raise the hem, but I fixed it good enough to get by, just for to-night."

The setting sun peeked into the window and filled the kitchen with bare, ugly light. I looked again at the hem of Mama's skirt and realized those glittery things were sta-ples.

"You look like Cinderella way, way, *way* before the ball!" I blurted, throwing my wet, wadded towel on the table. "I can't believe you'd let Burl make you wear sta-pled-together clothes!"

I ran angrily down the hallway, slamming my door behind me when I reached my room. I bounced onto my stomach on my bed and stuck my face into my pillow. I was afraid she'd come and knock on the door, but she didn't. When I heard her go out the trailer door I sat back up, yanked my notebook from my bookbag, and, shaking all over, began a letter to Mr. Amos.

Dear Mr. Amos,
    BOY, WERE YOU WRONG! You said this

could be a real adventure, remember, and we didn't have much to leave behind? Well, that creep Burl has Mama waitressing in a restaurant not half as good as Winstead's (in fact, it's a BAR, really) and kids here are even snootier than in K.C.—unless you count these two girls that everybody makes fun of. And one of them is even snooty. If I wasn't so polite I might have told her she

I stopped there because I suddenly remembered Mr. Amos couldn't read well enough to enjoy getting mail. I'd been with him a couple of times when his mail arrived, and he barely glanced at the envelopes and threw it in the trash.

I tore up the letter and put my head back down on my pillow, and listened to the hot, heavy silence of late-afternoon Gouge Eye.

Then I must have gone to sleep, because suddenly there was the sound of splashing and laughing and playful screaming and the *tha-PLUNK* of people bouncing on diving boards. "Hi, girls, can I take your order?" I turned in the direction of the voice to see my mother in her stapled-up uniform, crouched down beside the three girls lounging in neon bikinis behind the diving boards. "Hey, look you guys!" one of them called. "The mother of that girl with hairy arms and an attitude problem is waiting on us!"

My eyes jerked open and I sat bolt upright, my heart

slamming. It was totally dark, and Dierdre's face was in the sag of my screen, smashed far into it this time so she looked like the metal-faced lunatic in this gross horror movie Burl rented once. Her mouth was moving.

". . . waiting on us," she was saying. "Come on, Eliza, get up. It's time for hide and seek in Hilley's Woods."

"Leave me alone, I'm sleeping," I muttered, and flopped back down and over onto my stomach.

"You have to come. You're 'it' first, remember?"

"Oh, Dierdre," I grumbled, but got out of bed. Anything was better than taking a chance on falling back into that gross dream.

◆　◆　◆

Dierdre explained the rules of playing hide and seek in the woods to me as we walked through the soybeans, but I wasn't really concentrating. It seemed like regular hide and seek, except since it was dark you had to use a flashlight. After I counted to a hundred while everyone else hid, I got slightly confused and conked this kid named Max on the head with the flashlight when I saw him hunkering inside a nearby rotten log.

"You're 'it'!" I growled at him when he just hunched there, rubbing his head and looking bewildered. "Come out!"

"You can't just do that!" Dierdre practically yelled. "I told you, you have to shine the light on him and then beat him back to base. Anybody could find anybody if you could just whack them on the head that way, but you have to race back to base!"

49

I couldn't believe how worked up she was getting over this stupid baby game, when the humiliating afternoon at the pool hadn't seemed to bother her a bit.

"Hey, Dierdre, you're the one who dragged me out here, remember? I didn't even want to play this game, but you guys stuck me with being 'it' and I was nice enough not to protest!"

Meanwhile, Max got up, rubbed his head, and chugged through the trees. He reached base at the edge of the creek and started screeching, "Home free! Home free!"

I threw up my arms in disgust.

"Dierdre! Now see what you did with your stupid interrupting?" I cupped my hands around my mouth and furiously screamed through the woods, stomping my foot. "Max, you are tagged and you are now 'it,' period!"

"Yeah, Max!" Janelle piped from somewhere near me, with her little squeaky five-year-old's voice. She came out from behind a bush where she'd been hiding and put her head against my hip.

But Max just kept jumping up and down, all excited. In his mind he was home free to the point there was no reasoning with him.

"MAX, YOU ARE IT!" I screamed again.

A couple of the other kids wandered out of their hiding places and began milling around.

"What's going on?" Jay Roy whined down from a tree over our heads.

"You've got everything all messed up now," Dierdre

told me, speaking so calmly I wanted to slug her. "You better call the others out of their hiding places and start counting all over again while they hide all over again."

I turned to face her, my hands on my hips, practically shaking with anger.

"What difference does it make to you what I do, Dierdre? This is just about the stupidest baby game in the history of the universe, and you didn't even hide. You just kept standing around bugging *me*, so why are you blabbering about rules when you're breaking the number one rule, which is you have to hide if you're not 'it,' period, which you are not, now are you, Dierdre? Do you want to be 'it,' Dierdre? Because here's the stupid flashlight if you want to be 'it' so darn much!"

I threw the flashlight at her, and felt a little stab of guilt as Janelle flinched and moved a few inches away from me.

My chest felt like it was either going to explode or cave in as I began running full speed back through the soybeans, toward the dim little row of lights that marked where our houses huddled together like meek animals.

♦ ♦ ♦

"Wait up!" Dierdre called when I was almost through the soybeans. Since I was out of breath anyway, I did, but didn't give her the satisfaction of turning around. I swiped hard and quickly at my eyes with the tail of my T-shirt. When she came up even with me I saw she was dragging Janelle by the hand.

"Hey, really, Eliza. What's wrong with you?" she

asked. "Are you still mad at me about that attitude problem thing? Because I didn't mean anything by it. I just, you know, wondered."

Just then the mothers' voices started up, and Janelle dropped Dierdre's hand and began running toward the bait shop. A minute later Francy and Pete and Jay Roy and Max and the others barreled past us, too.

"No, I'm not mad about that," I said when we were alone, then took a deep breath and let it out. "Okay, Dierdre, I'll tell you what's wrong. Here we are, you and me, playing baby games in the woods and wearing cutoff jeans and cheap T-shirts. But meantime, the popular girls in Pertle Creek are probably sunbathing together on their patios, wearing neon swimming suits from a real clothing store, not somebody's garage sale, and listening to the radio. Not country and western, either. Rock stations, Dierdre! And I'll bet their yards aren't even weedy and filled with broken cars and worthless junk."

For a few seconds Dierdre didn't answer. Then, "But it's night, Eliza. How can they sunbathe at night?"

I let out a frustrated groan. "Not at night, in the afternoon! Don't you get the point, Dierdre? At night, they probably have parties—slumber parties, or even parties where they order store-bought pizza and invite boys! Or . . . or maybe they all go to the mall and then to a restaurant for cheeseburgers. Mr. Amos shouldn't have made me get my stupid hopes up. My mother will always be Cinderella without a fairy godmother, and we'll always be stuck with unreliable phones, and it's stupid to dream of things changing. Braggadocious old Burl is the only one allowed to have coming-true dreams and a fancy fresh start!''

She stood there silently sucking in her left cheek.

"Say something," I finally demanded.

"What's the matter with your phone?" she asked.

"Our phone?" An electric jolt fizzed through my veins.

"You said you're always stuck with unreliable phones."

The fizzing got worse, and I felt dizzy.

"You must have heard me wrong," I said. My voice seemed raw, like it was being scraped out of my throat. *Please just drop it,* I was thinking. *Please, Dierdre, just drop it.*

She squinted at me hard and expressionlessly for a few more seconds, then said in a solemn, even lower than usual voice, "I wanted you to come to the woods tonight because I want to show you something. Follow me."

CHAPTER
—7—

Show me something? Show me what?"

"Something I'm building," Dierdre said over her shoulder. She was walking back toward the woods, just assuming I was following her—which I was, mostly out of relief and gratitude that she'd dropped her phone questions.

She stopped at the edge of the trees, waiting for me to catch up. With her long legs she could walk through the tangled soybeans faster than I could run through them.

"It's in a cave about a quarter mile down the creek bank," she said. "It's not finished. Nobody else even knows I'm building it. You're the first."

Then she slipped into the woods, which suddenly seemed very dark and still, with all the kids and flashlights gone. The coyotes started howling, and I might have run on home if she hadn't said that last thing, that thing about me being the first.

"I can't see a thing," I grumbled, coming up behind her.

"Walk toe to heel, Indian style," she said. "You'll feel what's in front of you that way. You won't be as likely to step on a snake."

The water of the creek gleamed ahead of us, and when we reached it Dierdre turned left. I tried to stay right at her heels so if anyone was going to step on a snake it would be her. I forgot how upset I was supposed to be because it suddenly took every single bit of my concentration to keep up with her and not to trip and break my neck over the tangled undergrowth.

"See how the stars are blotted out above the treeline up ahead?" she said. "That's a big limestone bluff, and my cave is near the bottom of it."

Afraid to lift my eyes from my feet, I had to take her word for it. Then finally she cut left again, and the bluff loomed right in front of us like a huge ghost ship sailing suddenly from nightmare darkness. It was formed from light-colored stone that caused it to glow and even sparkle in places in the moonlight.

"Wow," I whispered.

"There's the cave," Dierdre said, pointing toward a little hole of darkness on the stone surface. The bluff seemed like a huge head, and the cave was like its open, surprised mouth.

"We're going . . . in there?" I asked, still whispering.

"Put your arms over your hair so the bats don't tangle in it," she instructed.

◆　◆　◆

It wasn't that I trusted Dierdre. It was just that she charged ahead on things and didn't give you a chance to complain, or talk reason, or back out. She seemed totally unselfconscious, in the strangest and truest sense of that word. She didn't seem to think about either danger or other people's opinions, period. That was so rare and weird in a person that it kept taking me by surprise, and left me so off-balance I was caught up in her wake like a paper boat rushing along through a fast-flowing muddy ditch.

Dierdre waited till we were in the cave, then pulled the flashlight I'd thrown at her from the waistband of her shorts.

"Duck," she ordered, and I quickly crouched down.

She clicked on the flashlight, and a wedge of squealing darkness peeled itself from the ceiling of the cave, broke into a hundred pieces, and zoomed over our heads and out the entrance.

"Besides the bats, there are also eyeless white salamanders in here. Unfortunately, you can't usually see them at night. They hide."

"Thanks for telling me, Dierdre," I muttered, nervously searching the shadowy, slimy floor of the cave. "Do they bite or anything?"

"They don't have eyes, remember? How could they bite what they can't see?"

"But they must bite something. They have to eat, don't they?"

She looked at me, frowning as though *I* was the one

I said those last two words accidentally. Maybe that awful close call about the unreliable phone had had something to do with it. Dierdre was crouching by the finished section of the raft, examining a knot in one of the ropes. As absorbed as she was in her work, I figured she'd let it pass, or maybe hadn't even heard.

"Before what?" she asked.

I stepped back into the shadows of the stone corridor. "Hey, we better go back," I said brightly.

She looked at me. "You said before. Before what?"

I turned so my back was to her and took a deep breath. "See, my dad got killed when I was in fourth grade. I kind of think of time as before then, and after."

I put my sunburned face against the cold, wet stone and closed my eyes. I was afraid Dierdre was going to ask in her flat, matter-of-fact way what that had to do with me not getting straight A's any longer, and I didn't have a clue how to even start to explain.

But she didn't.

"My father can't make a living here any longer and can't sell the house to have money to start up somewhere else," she said. I could hear her moving slightly, adjusting things. "He's gotten fed up and left us a couple of times, the last time for several months. I've spent a lot of time this summer imagining how never seeing my dad again would probably feel."

Really surprised, I opened my eyes and slowly turned back toward her. And my brain froze in horror—there

59

was a squiggle of movement on the floor a yard or so behind her back.

"Dierdre!" I screeched, jumping back, pointing to the puddle right behind where she squatted. She looked from me to the puddle, where the shallow water was suddenly churning. Then she stood up, picked up the flashlight, and walked calmly over to investigate.

"We're in luck! It's a pool of baby salamanders," she said, smiling as she focused the light on the puddle.

I crept up uneasily behind her, ready to run if I had to. The puddle teemed with creatures that looked like my little finger—curved, white and bald, eyeless.

"They'll never see," she whispered sadly. "They lived in the dark for so many thousands of years that they finally lost their eyes."

♦　♦　♦

We snuffed out the lantern and went home soon after that, leaving the salamanders to not even know the light had gone out.

The trailer was dark—my mother hadn't come home from Skeeter's yet. I remembered she'd told me to come and eat a burger, but I just couldn't face her right now. I was sorry I'd run away from her in the kitchen, but on the other hand I didn't want to have to look again at that stapled hem. It might make me mad enough to run away again, which probably meant I wasn't really all that sorry to begin with.

I ate some crackers and peanut butter, then decided I'd write a letter to Mr. Amos after all.

Dear Mr. Amos,

DO NOT THROW THIS LETTER AWAY!!! It's me, Eliza.

We are living in a pink trailer, but I AM HOPING Mama will see through Burl, that liar, and we'll be back in K.C. soon.

I'm sunburned (ouch!) because we went swimming today. Not Mama and me, but Dierdre, who is a strange, boylike, ax-swinging girl, and me. Well, actually, she uses the ax for her raft.

Have you found a sucker who will trade you a George Brett rookie card yet?

This Dierdre is my age. Unfortunately, she has the social graces of an eyeless salamander. By that I mean her hair is awful and she's been living here in the dark so long she doesn't notice when people (at the pool, for instance) think she's weird.

Well, I hope you didn't throw this away without reading it! If you did, then just ignore what I wrote (Ha! Ha!).

> *Your friend,*
> *Eliza Marie Branniman*

I put the letter in an envelope and wrote in large print on the front "DO NOT THROW THIS LETTER AWAY!!!"

I went to bed then, but lay thinking instead of sleeping, just like I had the night before.

This time I kept thinking of how I'd described Dierdre

in the letter. It really was pretty snooty of me to call her a salamander when she'd shown me, alone of all people, her raft.

And then, we'd also talked about our fathers—not much, but a little. I never talked about my father to anyone, ever.

Finally I got up, tore up the letter, and dropped the pieces in the wastebasket on top of the pieces of the other letter I'd started to write. While I was doing that I heard Mama coming up the three wooden stairs so I jumped in bed and pretended to be asleep.

CHAPTER

8

Mama had gone to work again when I woke up the next day, and the note waiting for me on the kitchen table had a definite no-nonsense tone to it.

> *Eliza, I am very sorry you were upset by my uniform, but honey, it is not Burl's fault it was a little too long. I hemmed it last night after work, you'll be pleased to know. Now, you come to Skeeter's for breakfast, PERIOD! I want to show you off to my new boss.*
>
> *Love and XXX—Me.*

I went back to my room and pulled on shorts and a T-shirt. I looked in the bathroom mirror and saw my heavy dark hair sticking to my head like it was glued there—all that chlorine in the swimming pool water yesterday had made it even mushier than usual. I scratched frantically at it, trying to make it look less like a dead cat, but I finally gave up and went outside.

Swishing through the dew still on the scraggly grass, I

peered at Dierdre's house through a crack between wood-piles. I could see Dierdre in her porch swing, reading her fat book. She turned her head in my direction.

"I'm going to Skeeter's," I called. It was the first time I'd had the nerve to strike up an out-of-the-blue conversation with anyone like that, but Dierdre didn't really seem to count. "My mother wants to show me off, ha, ha. I guess she's working there now, or something. Just for a day or two, till we move back to the city."

"I'll go with you," Dierdre called back.

◆ ◆ ◆

There were at least a dozen pickup trucks parked in front of Skeeter's, some with patient dogs lolling in the backs. Inside, a dark red counter ran like a scar along one side of the room, with bar stools pulled up to it covered in red plastic the exact color of scabs. Farmers, judging from their overalls, slouched on those scabbed-over stools, hunched with thick white coffee mugs between their hands.

More men sat in groups of four or five at the chrome tables filling the rest of the room. Each table was decorated with three dusty orange plastic flowers in an empty beer bottle. The air was smoky, and there was a deep loud buzz of talk and laughter. A radio was turned up loud to a country western station.

On one wall there was a pay phone, and on another wall was a purple neon clock advertising Budweiser—The King of Beers.

"There aren't any women in here," I whispered to Dierdre.

She shrugged. "Mrs. Ferguson hangs out here between customers at the bait shop, and there are a couple of women farmers in here right now that look like men because they're wearing overalls and they have their hair up under baseball hats." She paused to point these out, casually, with her elbow. "My mother and a few other women come in sometimes for a burger or to talk, but usually not in the morning when it's crowded and smoky and mostly farmers. And there's your mom, don't forget."

As if that was her cue to enter dramatically, Mama came out of the kitchen part of the restaurant just then, both hands filled with plates of bacon and eggs. With her orange hair and green eyes she looked beautiful even in Juanita's leftover waitressing uniform. She looked like she was outlined in black crayon and everybody else in the room was just outlined in pencil.

I noticed all the men at the counter turning their heads slightly in her direction. Then a short, muscular guy wearing a white T-shirt with the sleeves rolled up came out of the kitchen and let his dark eyes pass quickly over those men. They went back to their business, eating and slurping coffee and talking.

Just then, Mama saw me. She slapped the plates down on the counter with a clunk and waved both hands, jumping up and down.

"Eliza, Eliza! Come here, baby! Bring your new friend and come meet my boss!"

Dierdre hung back, but I had no choice but to slink over near enough for Mama to grab me and put her arm around my shoulders.

"Okay now, sweetie, this is Mr. Roger Skelton, the owner of this establishment. Roger, this is my daughter, Eliza Marie."

The guy with the white T-shirt and the dark eyes smiled and nodded, looking embarrassed to death. The other men at the counter squinted hard at their mugs, then a couple of them snorted and began turning bright pink with held-in laughter.

"Oh now, you boys stop that!" Mama scolded, hitting at a couple of the nearest men with the towel she'd had tucked into her apron. "I refuse to call this fine man by that awful nickname—Skeeter!—you all gave him when he was just a child, so you just better learn to live with that little fact of life."

Everybody laughed then, and with a wink at me, Mama picked up the two plates of food and went on about her work. She seemed much jokier than she ever seemed at Winstead's, where she was the only grown-up waitress and most of the customers were kids.

◆ ◆ ◆

"Your mother's beautiful," Dierdre said when we'd eaten and escaped from Skeeter's.

"Yeah," I agreed, "for all the good that's done her." I sat down on the curb across from the church and she sat down beside me. "Burl's a jerk, telling everybody lies about us. A jerk. She needs another princelike man like my dad was, someone to put her on a pedestal and make her life easy and perfect. You know, a rich or semirich businessman or plastic surgeon or something."

"So, your dad was rich?" Dierdre asked.

Just then a door slammed loud as a gunshot down the street, and we both whipped our heads in the direction of our houses. Dierdre stiffened as we saw her father go stomping past the woodpiles to jump in his truck. He slammed the door, then opened the passenger side door and kicked a bunch of beer cans onto the street. Then he slammed that door and peeled away.

Dierdre began agitatedly running her hands through her short, choppy hair, faster and faster, matting it up, spiking it in all directions. While she did this she was bumping her knees together like cymbals. She looked sort of like a big long-legged, wild-feathered bird.

"I'm going to work on my raft," she said, and stood up and walked quickly down the sidewalk.

Sighing, I put my chin in my hands and let my eyes rest on the sign in front of the church across the street. SUNDAY WORSHIP SERVICES 9:30 A.M. * * * REV. D. M. HARTSILL, PASTOR * * * REPENT! IT'S LATER THAN YOU THINK!

"Dierdre!" I yelled, an awful thought making me jump to my feet. "Dierdre, when does school start here?"

School in Kansas City didn't start till after Labor Day, which was over two weeks away.

67

"Next week," Dierdre called, turning to walk backward. "Three days from now."

Three Days? Three measly DAYS?

I guess that's when it all really sank in. Even if Mama saw the light and decided to dump Burl, we were probably too rooted in to leave within three measly days, especially with Mama having this new job and feeling so jokey about it and all. And Mama probably wouldn't leave after I was started in school, at least not for a semester.

There was a real possibility that this was my life now, not just a temporary adventure or catastrophe or whatever.

This was real!

I was trying to take in that fact when something big and red loomed in the corner of my left eye.

I turned toward it, squinted again down the block. A huge, shiny, cherry-red van had just pulled up in front of the trailer, and Burl was jumping from the double doors in the back. As I watched, my heart racing with anger, he began slinking carefully through the yard, then went slowly and on tiptoe up the wooden steps.

"Burl!" I screamed as he stood with his ear to the front door, listening. I ran as fast as I could down the block, across the street, and past the vacant lot. "Why are you sneaking around? For your information, Mama's not here. She's working!" I was dying to add, *At that stupid job you made her get!*

"Hey there, little missy," Burl said, looking flustered as I charged up to him. "Yes, well, I confess I knew your mother'd be at Skeeter's this morning, but I just needed to swing by and pick up a couple things."

He touched the brim of his hat and smiled uneasily as he slid on into the trailer, but I didn't smile back.

I didn't smile at the other Heartbreakers waiting there in the van, either, though they were looking my way and grinning and waving in a friendly way. I just sat there on the wooden stairs with my arms folded, glaring at them till Burl came slinking back out.

"I see you like the new wheels," Burl told me as he eased past me on the stairs. He was carrying a very lumpy black plastic garbage bag. "Cost us a small fortune, but it'll pay off in spades. Image is the important thing in this business, yes sirree, little missy. You can have all the talent under heaven, but style is the main thing."

I just glowered at him, and he touched the brim of his hat again and slunk back through the yard. He had his garbage bag slung like Santa's pack over his shoulder as he got into that gaudy, sleighlike van.

"Eliza, honey, tell your mama that I was here looking for her, and that I send her all my love, okay?" he called from the safety of his open window. "And, uh, would you tell her our gig will be lasting a little longer than we'd thought, so I'll see her in maybe about a few days or so?"

I didn't smile. "You just said you WEREN'T looking for her!" I yelled, rude or not.

The van took off with a jerk and a squeal, as if they thought I was going to throw something at them. I might have, too, if I'd had anything.

◆ ◆ ◆

"I just can't believe he didn't stop by the cafe," Mama said softly when I gave her Burl's message. "Or leave a note, or something. Shoot, I haven't laid eyes on the man since breakfast clear back yesterday."

"He took his cowboy boot collection," I told her. "Every last one of his boots is gone."

She'd been sitting at the kitchen table, rubbing the sides of her face, and her long, slender fingers stopped moving when I told her that. She closed her eyes and took a deep breath, then stood up and walked back into Burl's bedroom.

I sat at the table breaking toothpicks in half. I considered going in and telling her what I'd been trying to get a chance to tell her for two days, about all those lies Burl had told about us before we even got here. Then I could point out to her that it wasn't too late for us to move immediately back to Kansas City.

But then something dawned on me—we no longer had a pickup to move with! Burl had it with him, and had probably even used it as a down payment on that van! No Burl to load the heavy stuff up, either, for that matter.

Mama looked tired enough without laying another problem on her for no good reason, so I just kept those lies to myself.

But I put three toothpicks together and broke them all in one fell swoop, pretending they were Burl.

◆ ◆ ◆

That night, our third night in Gouge Eye, I lay in bed thinking again, harder than ever this time. Planning, really, more than thinking. I moved my head to the foot of the bed to catch the breeze from the window. There was now a faceprint where Dierdre kept sticking her head into the saggy screen, and it made the huge stars above Hilley's Woods look all squiggly, like a kindergartener had drawn them in the sky.

Okay, here were the facts.

Number one, Mr. Amos said I had a chance here to be whoever I wanted to be, though I wasn't sure he knew what he was talking about. Besides, number two, Burl had ruined that by lying and telling everybody that embarrassing thing about my having a so-called attitude problem. Yes, but, number three, he'd probably only gabbed about that here, in Gouge Eye. At Pertle Creek Junior High no one had ever heard of me yet. Except for Dierdre, who didn't really count, and who I somehow knew wouldn't tell anybody else what Burl had said.

Though I was furious at Burl, my hopeless mood from the swimming pool and the swimming pool dream the afternoon before had faded, and I could see I'd sort of overreacted when I'd felt so gloomy during hide and seek last night. When you sifted out the facts, what happened the first week of school was what counted, not one dinky little pool afternoon when people had their hair wet and didn't really recognize for sure who was who anyway. I still had a chance, one shot at being cool and popular and having people look up to me and treat me with respect. What happened when school started would probably be the most important thing, basically, that would ever happen to me. At least in junior high.

"You have one chance, so don't blow it," I said out loud.

My voice sounded solemn and windlike through the mesh of the screen, like I'd made an important and sacred vow.

CHAPTER
~ 9 ~

So I went with Dierdre to work on her raft the next day, since I was desperate now for information about school. As I watched her sawing and sanding, I asked her everything I could think of to ask, but her answers just frustrated me.

"Do a lot of the girls here go to salons to get their hair cut instead of their mothers cutting it? And how about clothes? They don't wear homemade or garage sale clothes much, do they? At least, the popular and semipopular girls don't. Right? I could tell that from their bathing suits."

"I don't know. I guess not," Dierdre said, after about a million years. All that time to think about it, then her answer didn't even make sense!

"You mean you guess not about salons, or not about homemade clothes, or not about mothers cutting their hair? Dierdre! I need to know this stuff!"

She shrugged and went on sanding. "I don't really

notice things like that," she said. "It doesn't seem important."

It doesn't seem important. That comment made me want to slap Dierdre—not once, but a whole bunch of times in a row, like people in movies slap somebody to bring them out of a trance.

"This move is a fresh start, a chance to make a run for what I want, Dierdre," I tried, patiently, to explain. "I'm just trying to think about my image and to do everything I can in advance. Burl says image is all-important and style is the main thing. People look up to you when you're stylish."

Dierdre rubbed at her jeans to get some of the sawdust off.

"I thought you told me Burl was a jerk," she said.

I rolled my eyes. "Burl *is* a jerk, but a stylish jerk who gets everything he wants!"

◆ ◆ ◆

The last days of that last schoolless week settled into a pattern. Burl stayed gone, I guess playing in Branson. Mama worked from morning till early evening at Skeeter's. Dierdre's angry father, Rick, came and went in his usual slamming and banging way. Hannah came over and cried on Mama's shoulder one night right after Rick slammed out. Other times, Mama would sit chewing one thumbnail and shaking her head sympathetically as their voices—Rick's yelling, Hannah's whimpering—poured through our three windows at night, drowning out the TV.

Dierdre was constantly at the cave, working on her raft. I went with her for someplace to go, but I pretty much gave up on pumping her for school information. Instead I took a notebook and sat on the creek bank just outside the cave, trying to plan and sketch my ideal wardrobe.

"What is that you're working on?" Dierdre asked when she finally noticed my notebook.

I looked up at her, where she stood sawdust-covered and sweaty, her hair in quivering spikes that appeared to be trying to escape from her head.

"I told you a couple of days ago, I'm doing some serious planning about my image. I want to make a good first impression at school."

"So you're drawing stuff?"

"Dierdre," I said with a sigh, "where image is concerned it's crucial that you have a perfect and cool look right off the bat. It's going to be tough, and I don't want to blow it."

"So you're drawing stuff?" she repeated, looking puzzled. "You mean, you're going to go out and buy all that stuff after you get it drawn?"

"Of course not! Where would I get that kind of money, Dierdre?"

She shrugged. "I thought maybe your dad was rich and you inherited his money. You said he was like a businessman or a plastic surgeon, remember?"

"Dierdre, I did not!" I slammed the notebook closed. "And just now I said I'm *planning!* Not buying, *planning!*"

Still she just stood there, squinty-eyed and frowning like when she was multiplying measurements in her head. "You obviously wouldn't understand," I told her. Suddenly I was absolutely furious with her, though I couldn't say exactly why. I jumped up, brushed off my shorts, and without even saying good-bye to her, stomped on home.

◆ ◆ ◆

On Sunday afternoon, Hannah invited Mama and me to a barbecue in their front yard to celebrate school starting the next day.

It wasn't, of course, like a real barbecue, like you see on commercials on TV. It wasn't, for instance, on a patio, and Hannah didn't serve steaks, or even hamburgers. She served hot dogs, potato chips, and Kool-Aid.

There were three lawn chairs set up in the brown grass, and Hannah, Mama, and Rick sat in those. The seats were partly frayed out and I wondered if Rick would fall through his, onto the little hill of beer cans that were mounting up on the grass under him. Dierdre sat in the porch swing, reading her fat book, and I sat cross-legged on the little sidewalk that bisected their yard.

Things went okay until the adults began a boring conversation about B. J. Turley and the weekly auction he held in the old bank building.

"B.J. sometimes has antiques," Hannah told Mama. "And collectibles, such as old Coca-Cola bottles."

"A buncha old junk," Rick said, and belched. He took a last long drink from the beer in his hand, and threw the can toward the rusty For Sale sign near the woodpiles.

Hannah went to the little card table they were using for a picnic table, picked up the Kool-Aid pitcher and began scurrying around refilling our paper cups. "Now, hon," she said softly to Rick, "there's junk, true, but sometimes there's more good things than you can shake a stick at."

"Why does everybody say that—'shake a stick at'?" Dierdre asked, raising her eyes from her book. "Where's that expression come from?"

Everybody ignored her question. That evening it was hot, hot—way too hot for Dierdre's brain-strain questions. Mama was still in her waitressing uniform from Skeeter's, and she lifted up the little white apron and began fanning her face with it. I twisted my thick, sticky hair into a tight knot to keep it off my neck.

"Can you believe it? Next week B.J.'s gonna try to auction off the old Tucker's Grocery building," Rick suddenly said, then snarled a mean-sounding laugh.

Mama immediately quit fanning. "Really?" she asked in a breathless way that made me turn to look directly at her.

"He's just hoping for a fool to happen along," Rick muttered, and flicked the ash of his cigarette into his paper cup. He stared at the rusty For Sale sign hanging in their yard. "As if anybody would move to this little rathole town to start up a store. Every day I break my danged back cutting wood which I can't get a decent price for. There's good jobs going begging in the Saint Louis paper, but this here house I can't sell will have me stuck in this one-horse town till the day I die."

He suddenly jumped up and kicked over his lawn chair. "If somebody'd just set this place on fire so's I could get ahold of the insurance money they'd be doing me a big favor," he growled. "If I had the gumption, it's what I'd oughta do myself!"

He stalked up the porch stairs and into the house, slamming the screen door hard behind him.

"I'm going to the creek," Dierdre said, so quickly and quietly I barely heard. Still holding her fat book, she slipped off the porch and took off at a run.

"Oh, dear," Hannah breathed, watching Dierdre go. She stood very straight and still, holding that pitcher of red Kool-Aid while the hot wind pushed her dress against her legs. She looked like an ancient stone statue of an Egyptian queen, carefully carrying a precious sacrifice. In fact, she was so pale that you might have thought she was actually a statue like that, if her eyes hadn't been filling with real live tears.

Mama jumped up and went to put an arm around her shoulders.

"I'll go find Dierdre," I said, eager to get out of there before Hannah started crying for real.

◆ ◆ ◆

As I knew she would be, Dierdre was at the cave. She was crouched in the shadows just outside it, her back against the cool stone of the bluff.

"You okay?" I asked her.

She shrugged and didn't answer. Finally she said, "I hate it when he talks crazy about fire, wishing the house would burn so he could get the insurance money for it. I can't stand that. That's one thing I just can't stand, and he does it all the time now, practically every time he's drunk."

I sat down beside her, pulled my knees up to my chest and rested my cheek on them.

I scrunched shut my eyes because my heart suddenly felt squeezed till it almost hurt. I understood what she was feeling much better than she suspected.

"I hate fire, too," I heard myself say. "My father died in a fire. He worked in a fireworks factory. There was an explosion."

Dierdre slid down so she sat next to me instead of crouching. I suspected she might be looking at me so I opened my eyes and looked back at her.

"That must have been horrible," she said quietly. "I can see why you think of time as before that happened, and after."

I nodded, swallowing. I was glad she understood that, glad somebody did, but I couldn't say anything else right then.

It was getting dark. We just silently watched the water slide like a black snake through the darkness for a long time.

CHAPTER
~10~

The next day, school started.

Charlie, our bus driver, picked Dierdre and me up in front of her house. It was hot already by 7:30—more like the middle of July than the very end of August. By the time Charlie swung the bus around the sleeping dogs on Main Street and pulled onto the road to Pertle Creek, sweat and the wind coming in our window had made the right half of Dierdre's hair prickle straight up.

My own heavy hair was clinging to my neck, and I shook it off with a shiver of irritation. I felt jittery enough to begin with, and it was really getting on my nerves that Dierdre was so calm she was almost zombielike.

"Well, here we go!" I said, and rolled my eyes elaborately, trying to spark a little fear or at least interest on her part. "Junior high is certainly going to be different."

"From what?" she asked.

"Dierdre! From our lives up till now! At this very moment we're traveling toward our entire future! And what happens right at the beginning, these first days, will set the pattern!''

She frowned but didn't speak. I had no idea how to get across to her how important it was for our images that we make the right kind of first impression—definitely not like we'd made at the swimming pool.

"One side of your hair's sticking up," I told her, and as she pawed at it I sighed and looked down at my new jeans.

Mama and I had gone shopping for school clothes back in July, to catch a sale they were having at Wal-Mart. She said we could spend fifty dollars, which sounded like a fortune, but to my surprise it only amounted to two pairs of jeans and two T-shirts. I'd been saving all four things carefully. I hadn't worn any of them even once. I had, though, washed the jeans three times to break them in, but still they were stiff, not like designer ones, which I knew would feel soft right off the bat, like you'd worn them forever. Besides the new jeans, I was now wearing the new pink T-shirt. Unfortunately I'd tucked it in when I put it on before deciding the waist of the new jeans came up a little too high for tucked-in shirts to look cool, so the bottom of the shirt was slightly wrinkled. Also, it seemed a little boxy, not tucked in.

Actually neither this type of jeans nor the T-shirts would have made the ideal wardrobe list I'd been planning and sketching, but at least I wasn't wearing a faded, outgrown sundress to school, like Dierdre was.

Just then a pair of scissors—the rounded-edge kind

that the little kids use—whizzed across our seat back, sailing neatly between our two heads.

"Jay Roy, you settle yourself down!" I yelled toward the back of the bus, where all three of Gouge Eye's fourth-grade delinquents-in-training were sharing a seat. "You could have cut our heads off! Or slit one of our jugular veins!"

Giggles rose from the seat where Jay Roy, Max, and Timmy slumped out of sight, except for a fringe of messy hair.

"Next time we *will* slit your juggling vein!" Jay Roy piped.

"Don't give them ideas," Dierdre advised.

◆ ◆ ◆

Like I'd suspected from the pool that day, everyone at Pertle Creek Junior High clearly seemed to belong to a certain group. Everyone, that is, except Nancy Petrinsen.

"Well, there you two are," she said, sliding in between Dierdre and me as we waited in the cafeteria line at lunch. "I promise to forgive you for not waiting up, just don't let it happen again."

Dierdre smiled, but I just couldn't. I felt slightly nauseous, partly from Nancy's smell (she didn't use deodorant yet, and *needed* to). I kept my head tilted down, and pretended to read the nutrition information on the milk carton in my hand as I inched away from her. She was chattering up at Dierdre and didn't even seem to notice.

Nancy ended up eating with us, but I told myself it

could have been worse. At least she wasn't in any of my classes.

◆　◆　◆

All three of the girls from behind the diving board were in my last-hour English class. I'd wondered if I'd recognize them in school clothes, and it turned out to be easy— three swingy-haired girls with wonderful outfits sitting together by the big windows at the back left corner of the room.

I watched the cool, slightly bored way they ran their eyes over everyone else in the room. That was exactly how they'd looked around at people all afternoon at the pool that day. Amanda, Casey, and Lauren—I wrote their names on my left hand when Mrs. Hogelman called role.

Dierdre and I had seats in the back of the room in that class too, only on the opposite side from the windows, near a bunch of boxes of books that were labeled "To Be Recycled." Still, by leaning to my left I could see Amanda pretty clearly, and she was the most important to watch because she had the best hair. It swung out from her head when she bent to write something. It hung straight and shiny, down just below her chin, and little lines of sunlight moved up and down it.

There was a big picture of William Shakespeare on the wall right beside me, so a couple of times I whipped around to catch my reflection unawares in the glass. I hoped, of course, that my hair would be swinging.

It didn't swing, though. It just huddled there, dark and

nearly as shapeless as Shakespeare's own weird hair, and my face peered from inside it like a glob of dough.

◆ ◆ ◆

On the bus going home, I tried again to talk seriously to Dierdre, who was, at least, considerably more talkative than she had been that morning. In fact, she was absolutely gabby, but she didn't want to talk about anything important.

"Dierdre, I don't want to sound snooty, but we can't sit by Nancy at lunch tomorrow. Okay? We have to think about first impressions. We don't want to look like people who have to just take whatever's left, friendwise."

"My raft will be just perfect for the science project we're doing in Mr. Thurber's class," she said as though she hadn't heard me, sticking her hands in her armpits and hugging herself. "I can use the data I've already collected about water and wind conditions at the creek, and once the raft is seaworthy I can tether it in the current and take more complicated measurements from the water speed and depth, and then correlate all the data into . . ."

"Seaworthy?" I said, and snorted, annoyed that she hadn't been listening. "Come on, Dierdre, I wouldn't exactly call your raft 'seaworthy.' 'Creekworthy' would be more like it."

I felt ashamed the minute I'd said that, but Dierdre was too wound up to notice it was a put-down.

"Whatever," she said. "Listen, I'll need your help in a couple of days to pull the raft out of the cave and test it, okay? Then I can leave it tethered in the water, and maybe even add studies of the various fish and amphibians to my . . ."

"Amphibians? You mean the measly little frogs in Twisted Creek? Dierdre, will you wake up! There's more to life in seventh grade than dazzling the teachers with stuff like science projects, okay? Much, much more!"

I think I may have yelled that, because she stopped talking and so did everyone else on the bus. I stared at the bookbag in my lap, waiting for the noise and confusion to start again.

"There are also several species of salamanders and newts in Twisted Creek," Dierdre said stiffly, clearly offended.

I looked imploringly into her eyes. "Dierdre, didn't it bother you that we didn't really talk to anyone in our classes today?"

"We talked to each other. We're in all the same classes but two."

"But we're not in a group! A group is at least three, and Nancy Petrinsen doesn't count. A group looks like it belongs together because it shares a certain image."

Suddenly I was far too exhausted to continue this frustrating conversation. I slid down in my seat, put my knees against the metal backrest in front of me, and closed my eyes.

"So what are *you* doing for your science project?" Dierdre asked a minute later.

We had till the end of the week to even pick a project, and another week to turn it in. Thinking about science projects this early was so seriously uncool that anyone but Dierdre would have been embarrassed to death asking another person such a question.

But I wasn't in the mood to explain all that, and I was afraid if I just told her I hadn't decided she'd start right in giving me a bunch of suggestions. So I groped through my mind and came up with a quick answer.

"I think I'll grow a crystal garden with this kit I bought in Oklahoma a few years ago. It's got crystal-growing chemicals, for rubies and sapphires and stuff. It's even got test tubes and a graduated cylinder."

"So you're just using a kit?" she asked, sounding very unimpressed.

CHAPTER
~11~

When we got off the bus I said good-bye to Dierdre and went on home. Mama had her sewing machine set up on the kitchen table and was messing with Juanita's old waitressing uniform, probably taking in the sides. She took her foot off the pedal and stopped right in midstitch when I came through the doorway.

"Well hi, sweetie, how was junior high?" she asked cheerfully. "Did you make lots of new friends?"

I could tell from the look in her eyes that she was dying for me to say yes and be all smiley and everything. But she made it sound like you could make friends as easily as you made paper dolls, and I just couldn't cope with that right then.

"I guess," I mumbled, shrugging. I hurried on down the hall and into my turtle-shell room, where I threw my bookbag on the bed and rummaged in my closet till I found my crystal garden kit. I was looking at the picture on the box when I heard Mama push back her chair and come toward me down the hall.

"Oh, that crystal kit," she said softly from my doorway. "I remember so well that trip we took to visit my cousins in Oklahoma City. You and your dad spent three whole days at the science center there while Doris and Sue and I shopped our heads off."

"The Omniplex," I whispered. "It was called the Omniplex."

"He bought you this kit in the gift shop there. I was almost mad at him when I saw it." She sat down beside me and gently touched the box. "It was so expensive, and far too complicated for an eight-year-old. But he said . . . he said he could help you. He said, 'Lorna Jean, we'll work on this together, my girl and me.' And then, of course, he never . . . got the chance."

"I can handle it myself now, so I guess I'll use it as my science project," I said quickly, not lifting my eyes.

I remembered it was the picture on the box I'd loved. Those glistening rubies, those diamonds, that bright blue sapphire. I wanted them. Not making them, but just the thought of owning them was what had me clinging to Daddy's legs there in the Omniplex, begging, hopping up and down.

"I think your dad's favorite thing in the world was to watch you learn something new," Mama said. Her voice sounded sad, but somehow I could tell she was also smiling. "When you were in kindergarten, for instance, I kept kneeling down to tie your shoes all the time. But your dad would never do that. Instead, each time he'd see your shoe untied he'd pull you onto his lap and patiently show you how to do it and watch as you tried, and tried, and tried, until finally you got the hang of it."

I heard her sniff a couple of times, then she bent and kissed the top of my head. "This crystal kit would have been like that, Eliza. He would have gotten such a kick out of seeing you learn from it."

She went back out to her sewing then, and I took the lid off the box and stared at the ingredients and instructions inside. There were several small jars with tight lids, each lid with a string suspended from inside it. There were eight chemical packets labeled ALUM, three labeled RUBY, and one labeled SAPPHIRE. I'd heard of rubies and sapphires, of course, but not alums. Alum crystals, the directions said, were the easiest to grow, while sapphires and rubies were grown "with some difficulty by the beginner."

I looked again at the picture on the box, and for the first time noticed the boy and girl were holding up the rubies and sapphires, admiring them, smiling, but they were totally ignoring the clear crystals on the table as though the alums, the things I'd once thought were diamonds, were stupid and hadn't really been worth the effort.

I slid off the bed and got busy, carefully following the instructions, filling the jars with warm water exactly measured with the graduated cylinder, dissolving the chemicals, one packet in each jar. The little strings hung down into the murky water, and you were supposed to rotate the jar till no chemical junk settled on the bottom. You were supposed to rotate each jar a couple of times daily, in fact.

Crystals would start forming within hours, and would keep growing for about a week.

I got totally caught up in putting the crystal garden together that night, arranging and rearranging the jars, rotating them, then rotating them some more when chemicals started to settle to the bottom. A couple of times I could feel Mama watching from the doorway, but I was concentrating too much to stop and talk.

◆ ◆ ◆

I woke the next morning to a dazzle of light from where I'd lined up the twelve small jars along my deep window-sill. I bounced onto my knees for a closer look and saw the eight baby alums already growing up a storm in all direc-tions. The three baby rubies were slightly started, too. The string in the single sapphire jar seemed totally bare. I was squinting at it when Dierdre suddenly stuck her head in the screen.

"You started your crystal garden!" she said, leaning farther in to inspect the jars.

"What time is it?" I asked, rubbing my eyes.

"Uh, time for the bus I think," she mumbled without looking up from the crystals.

"Dierdre! Thanks a lot for telling me!"

I jumped off the bed, threw on the clothes I'd luckily laid out the night before, and barely made it outside as the bus was pulling to our curb.

◆ ◆ ◆

It seemed even hotter and more humid than it had been the day before, and the bus ride and then the schoolday itself went by in a fuzzy blur of heat. I didn't even have the energy to think of a way to dodge Nancy at lunch, so she sat with us again.

In fact she changed her schedule and transferred into our last-hour English class. She flopped down in the vacant seat right in front of Dierdre as if she owned the place.

By 2:00, when that class started, the heat was just unreal and everybody was pretty much out of it. Two boys right in front of me kept comparing the slime trails their sweaty elbows left as they slid across their desks. Once in a while somebody would peel their thighs from their chair, and everyone would laugh at the sound. Mrs. Hogelman evidently wasn't feeling too perky herself and gave us the hour to begin a how-to paper, which she said we should turn in tomorrow. She sat at her desk while we supposedly worked on this, pressing tissue after tissue to her throat and forehead and occasionally making miserable little sighing noises.

I couldn't think of a topic for my paper, so I watched across the room as this cute boy named Russell Harris flirted with Amanda and Lauren and Casey. Russell had big wet circles under his arms, but they didn't bother me on him like they did on Nancy Petrinsen. Russell pretend-tried to grab Casey's paper off her desk, but she snatched it up and held it tight against her chest. Amanda and Lauren scooted their desks closer to Casey's, and the next time Russell lunged, all three girls huddled together guarding the paper and silently giggling.

I shoved my damp hair off my forehead and looked over at Dierdre. She was sucking her pencil and frowning intensely at her paper, which was nearly covered with her tiny neat handwriting.

Nancy was busily erasing things with a wet-looking, chewed-on eraser, then smearing the rubber eraser droppings all over her desk. I could hear her breathing through her mouth. Then suddenly she turned to glare at the popular girls and hoisted herself to her feet.

"Casey and Lauren and Amanda are fooling around and not working on the assignment, Mrs. Hogelman," she said.

My stomach clenched with misery as Amanda shot Nancy a dirty look that took in everything and everyone in our corner of the room, including me.

"People, now, let's be busy," Mrs. Hogelman said limply, reaching for another tissue.

Nancy grunted with satisfaction and sat down, as my neck burned hot with humiliation.

◆　◆　◆

"What are you writing your paper about?" Dierdre asked when the bell finally rang.

Tiny drops of perspiration dotted her top lip. I figured she was just asking me so I'd ask her back.

I shrugged. "What are you?"

"How to identify trees by their bark," she answered.

I went on shoving books into my bookbag and looked down at the white rectangle on my desk. I picked up my paper. To my complete surprise, I had written on it as I watched Russell flirt with Casey. I'd put a title across the top line—HOW TO BE POPULAR IN SEVENTH GRADE.

Dierdre was craning her neck over to see, but I stuck the paper quickly in my bookbag.

"It says, 'How to Make Pottery in Seven Shades,'" Nancy Petrinsen told Dierdre, then, without looking at me at all, sashayed down the aisle, her busybody nose in the air.

"I didn't know you could make pottery," Dierdre said. My head ached. "It's not that hard," I told her.

◆ ◆ ◆

The bus was stifling as we sat waiting for everyone to board. Dierdre pulled out her how-to paper to work on. I put my forehead on the window and stared out, wondering if my brain was melting. Amanda and Casey and Lauren were walking down the sidewalk together, toward a big white car that was idling by the curb, waiting to pick them up. There was elegant cursive writing along the back of the car, a silver stream of letters reading LINCOLN CONTINENTAL.

"Do you think life is like a candy bar and you can pretty much pick it out, or more like measles and it's something you just get and are stuck with?" I asked, turning toward Dierdre.

She stopped writing, looked at me, and shrugged. "The teachers say you can be anything you want. Even president, or an astronaut."

"And you believe them?"

"Of course," she said immediately, looking a little

shocked at the question. "Why wouldn't I? They're teachers."

The elegant car containing Amanda, Casey, and Lauren pulled smoothly from the curb. The windows were up, so it was evidently air-conditioned. Mama and I had never had an air-conditioned car, not that we had any car at all, at the moment.

◆ ◆ ◆

"Is Burl's new van air-conditioned?" I asked Mama at supper that night.

She quit twirling the spaghetti noodles on her fork and looked quickly up at me. "What new van?"

"You know, the one he and the Heartbreakers had when he stopped by to pick up his boots, the cherry-red one. Didn't I . . . tell you about it?"

She dropped her fork down on her plate.

"New as in 'new,' Eliza, or new as in 'just not very used'?" she asked quietly.

"New as in 'new,' " I answered truthfully. "Why?"

She bit her bottom lip, took several deep breaths, then picked up her garlic bread and stuffed it into her iced tea glass. She screeched her chair back, jumped up, and started pacing.

"So, he needs me to earn some money, he says." Her voice was a whisper, but she was gesturing wildly with her hands. "So we can hurry up and get the band squared up solid and make some permanent plans, he says! For necessary expenses, he says! So I work and keep house so he can gallivant around Branson and drop in when he feels like

94

it, and he buys a new van but can't see his way clear to spend a measly buck or two on a phone call!"

She stopped by the table and stood helplessly glowering down at our food, waving her hands around. Then she snatched up her tea glass, ran across the kitchen, hurled the tea and garlic bread into the sink and switched on the garbage disposal.

"So there, take that, Burl Harley Hawkins!" she exclaimed, though you could barely hear her above the crunch and heave of the semibroken garbage disposal.

"Mama? Are you okay?"

She looked at me, her eyes too bright and her face pale. "I will not cry about this, Eliza," she said. "I'm going for a walk, but don't worry. I need to burn off some anger, honey, but I will not go to pieces over that man."

And then she left. I watched out the kitchen window as she stormed down the sidewalk, her head up, her elbows stabbing the air, her pretty hair igniting the twilight sky, matching the sunset that was flaming over Hilley's Woods.

I cleaned up the kitchen and couldn't avoid listening to Dierdre's father yelling next door. I wondered, in junior high, had he pictured himself cutting wood for a living? I heard the quiet, sobbing protests of Dierdre's sweet mother, who'd dreamed of being a veterinarian but was doomed to be a yelled-at wife and mother instead. And my own mother—what were the dreams of her heart? Surely not living in a hot, bubble-gum pink trailer. Mr. Amos, too, smart as he was, must have once pictured better things for himself than being a janitor in a run-down apartment building. If they could have been any-thing, like the teachers said everybody could, why hadn't any of them picked something decent, instead of settling for being . . . big nothings? Where had they all gone wrong?

My heart was pounding and I was breathing fast with determination by the time I'd washed the last of the dishes. If I didn't do something drastic *right now,* people were going to start associating me with gross, obnoxious Nancy, and it would be all downhill from there.

I yanked open the utility drawer and stood staring down at Mama's good scissors. I picked them up and felt power climb up my arm as my hand wrapped around their cool black handles.

I went to my room and stood in the doorway for a few seconds, watching the beautiful baby rubies as they care-fully formed themselves into gems that put the silly, fast-growing and gangly alums to shame.

Then before I could lose my nerve, I ran into the bathroom and locked the door.

CHAPTER
~12~

You cut your hair," my mother said the second I came into the kitchen the next morning. "Oh, Eliza, you cut your hair . . . a lot."

"No one's wearing it long this year," I explained.

"Oh," she said. The eggs she was cooking were sizzling, turning brown and rubbery around the edges. The spatula in her hand, I noticed, dripped bacon grease onto the worn linoleum floor.

"Those are going to burn," I pointed out.

But she didn't seem to hear. She licked her lips. "I guess maybe Hannah could even it up some," she said. "She told me she cuts Dierdre's hair herself."

"I already did that! I spent a whole hour evening it up over and over again last night. That's why it's maybe pretty much shorter than I started out to cut it. What's the matter? Don't you like it?"

Before answering, she took the frying pan from the stove and walked over to the door with it. She shoved the door open with her shoulder, and threw the burned eggs outside.

"It's . . . choppy," she said then, staring down at the splattered eggs on the ground and not turning to look at me. "Or something."

"You just don't know the style, Mama!" I said, though my heart was slamming in my chest now, and it was almost hard to talk normally. "It's cut exactly like Amanda Chesselmyer has hers this year. Exactly!"

She turned toward me, and her face looked, I don't know—tight or something. Her chin was trembling, too.

"Chesselmyer? I saw that name in big gold letters on the door of the bank when I opened up my account. Eliza Marie, I suppose the daughter of the president of the Pertle Creek Community Bank and Trust can afford to get herself a thirty-dollar haircut, which yours certainly is not."

I felt panic rushing toward me then, and anger too. It was her fault, not mine, that we didn't have haircut money! I wanted to remind her that *she* had been the one to probably give Burl her salary for that lousy toupee and that stupid cherry-red van, not me. Then I wanted to run into my room and slam the door. But she beat me to it. She ran into her own room and slammed the door, leaving me standing there alone in the burned-egg smoke of the hot kitchen. A couple of cats were fighting over the eggs outside.

"Shut up!" I yelled down to them out the window. "Shut up, up, up, you hear me?"

They looked up at me with confused expressions on their faces. I ran to the bathroom, and stood breathing hard and staring desperately in the mirror.

It was true that the job of cutting my hair had been much harder than I'd anticipated. Amanda's hair looked puffy and smooth on top and curved just below her chin, but mine wanted to do kind of the opposite—curve inward to hug my head on top and then puff out along my chinline.

Still, it was pretty much the right length, so it surely looked okay. I reminded myself that it was hard to judge your own appearance, much less your daughter's since mothers were too old to know the styles.

I took several deep breaths to calm down, closed my eyes, and forced myself to open them and look again in the mirror, honestly and frankly.

And I nearly died of relief. It was so obvious!

Yes, something was wrong. Yes, Mama had had a reason after all to be upset with my new appearance.

But it wasn't the hairstyle itself. It was just that it was off my shoulders now, and left far more of my skin exposed, and on every inch of that skin grew those awful, wiry dark hairs! They'd driven me crazy all my life, but now they were really disgusting, and it was definitely time to do something about them.

I grabbed the disposable razor Burl had left in one of the empty holes in the toothbrush holder. It was slightly caked with gross stuff, but I easily rinsed most of that out.

After I'd shaved my arms from my wrists to my elbows, the top, less hairy part between my elbows and shoulders went much more quickly. I was just replacing Burl's razor when I heard the bus, so I grabbed my books from the kitchen and made a run for it. Charlie had been pulling away from the curb, but he saw me running and stopped and swung the door back open.

"G'morning, E . . .Eliza," he said.

"Good morning," I answered, smiling the kind of polite but not-too-friendly smile Amanda and Casey and those guys used for people not in their crowd. I could tell he was surprised by my new look. I guessed that's how it would be all day—everybody surprised and impressed.

The bus, as I walked through, was quieter than I'd ever heard it. I wondered if something bad had happened, like somebody's dog being hit and killed on the road.

Jay Roy jumped up onto the seat he shared with Max and Timmy, stepping all over their hands in the process. "Wow, she's been in a fight!" he yelled as his two friends moaned in pain and slugged at his legs. "Looks like Ninja karate whacks! Or else alien laser guns!"

Ignoring him, I slid in beside Dierdre, who flinched away from me, her back flat against the window and her eyes round and wide.

"Eliza, what happened?" she said in a scared-sounding rush. "Was it one of the dogs? Did they knock you down into the brambles? Don't you think you should go home and . . . I don't know, bandage yourself?"

The squeaky tone of her usually low, flat voice made me realize my arms were burning. Looking down, I saw that they were crisscrossed with scratches, some of them oozing little red lines.

I felt sick, but the bus was barreling along the highway to Pertle Creek, and it was too late to ask Charlie to turn around and take me back. Thank goodness I had a sweater in my new locker at school—one the person who'd had the locker last year had left behind.

I looked directly at Dierdre, trying not to panic.

"Oh, Dierdre, please, I just have to know. Please!" I whispered, grabbing her skirt so hard my knuckles ached. "Except for these scratches and cuts, I look really good this way, right? Aren't I right about that? I mean, picture the scratches healed and my arms all smooth and hair-less."

She just stared at me, her mouth slightly open.

"Dierdre! You're the one who told me everybody could be anything, remember? This is a new, improved look! A makeover!"

She looked directly back at me for a few seconds longer. "Your hair looks triangular," she said, squinting like she was analyzing a hard math problem. "You know, pointed on top and wide at the sides, like an isosceles triangle— like a Christmas tree."

"*Dierdre, it does not!*" I pretty much screamed. Charlie glanced up at us in his rearview mirror, so I took a deep breath and remembered that this was Dierdre talking, and certainly not a fashion expert. I calmed myself down. "Dierdre, listen. This is cool hair. This is exactly the style Amanda and those guys are wearing this year. Exactly."

Again, she looked directly back at me for a few seconds, but this time I saw something strange that I couldn't quite figure out slide into her eyes. I figured it might be some newfound glimmer of fashion awareness.

But then she said, "Oh." She took her fat book out and opened it. She began reading and totally ignored me, which was fine with me. Trying to talk to Dierdre about fashion was like trying to talk to a dog about nuclear physics.

CHAPTER
—13—

I made a beeline for my locker when the bus got to the school, and put on the scratchy sweater that, thank goodness, was still wadded up under some junk on the floor.

That day was as blisteringly hot as the ones before it, so, needless to say, I was miserable and got more miserable by the minute. My arms soon reached the stage where I couldn't tell if they hurt or itched. All I knew was that my brain was about to explode through my skull, and after every class I ran to the nearest rest room, yanked off the sweater, and stood for a couple of minutes inside one of the stalls with wet paper towels draped over both arms from wrists to shoulders.

Dierdre followed me to the rest room after science, the first morning class we had together.

"I don't exactly need an escort, you know," I told her. I figured she'd make some crack about the gob of paper towels I was jerking from the dispenser, but she didn't.

I had a close call the time after third period, which was math. When I had just started wetting the paper towels,

I heard a loud burst of hall noise that meant somebody else was coming into the rest room. I grabbed the towels from the sink and dove into one of the stalls and quickly slammed the metal door, leaving a thick trail of drips behind me.

I was pretty sure the new voices in the room belonged to eighth graders.

"Oh, gross, my hair is wilting! Hand me your spray, Heather."

"Use all you want. It's the ninety-nine-cent-a-can kind."

"Everybody's hair is flat and wilting. It's so hot your make-up about slides right off onto the floor."

"Did you guys see that little seventh grader wearing a *sweater*? A *sweater*! And her *hair!*"

"I know! It looked like she cut it herself, in the dark or something. Seventh graders are just *so* weird!"

They all laughed. I closed my eyes and held my breath and moved farther back, hoping they wouldn't somehow see my feet and recognize me. I thought about standing up on the toilet till they left, but they might wonder why a closed stall had no feet showing under it. They might even yank open the door or crawl under or something, and *then* what would I do?

The hair spraying seemed to go on forever. When they finally went out, I ran into the hall and gulped air.

♦ ♦ ♦

The rest of the morning, I didn't feel so good. I mean, I was nauseous and depressed at that overheard conversation now, instead of just scratchy and smothering and itchy.

At lunch Nancy wedged herself between Dierdre and me as we sat to eat.

"Your hair is disgusting that way, Eliza," she informed me. "It makes your chin look practically double."

I looked at her. She was gulping her chocolate milk through two straws, filling her cheeks with it before swallowing so they looked like twin water balloons.

My stomach began churning. "Excuse me," I mumbled, and got up and hustled to the rest room, where I hid in the same stall I'd hidden in earlier. I stood there with my eyes closed, taking deep breaths. What could be worse than having Nancy Petrinsen think *you* were the disgusting one?

♦ ♦ ♦

When I finally pulled myself together enough to leave the rest room and went on to my afternoon classes, I told myself things surely wouldn't get any worse.

But right at the beginning of English class last hour, Mrs. Hogelman asked us to hand in our how-to papers.

I felt stunned. I'd forgotten the assignment completely.

I looked over at Dierdre. She was tapping several papers into a neat stack and fastening them with a paper clip. She looked up at me and smiled. It figured that neatly paper-clipping an assignment together would be the kind of thing that made Dierdre feel happiest.

I returned her smile with a grimace of pure panic.

"Didn't you write about making pottery?" she whispered across the aisle.

"I . . ."

I meant to tell her that with the hair cutting and everything, I had simply forgotten to do the assignment. But for some reason, that isn't what came out of my mouth.

". . . left my paper at home," I whispered sadly back.

"Eliza, are we having some problem?" Mrs. Hogelman asked, tilting her chin down and looking toward me over the rhinestones along the tops of her glasses.

"Yes, ma'am," I said. "I . . . sort of left my paper accidentally at home or . . . or maybe slightly didn't finish it . . . or something."

My voice trailed to a squeak near the end. I'd discovered in midsentence that though I evidently could fib to Dierdre, I couldn't quite fib to a teacher.

A few people giggled and I felt the burning in my arms stretch clear up through my neck. A tiny bug—one of those silverfish that comes out in the fall—was lying on his back a few feet from me, kicking his legs helplessly in the air. I knew just how he felt.

"Let's talk about it after class," Mrs. Hogelman said.

◆ ◆ ◆

"Eliza, I must say I'm a tad concerned about you."

Mrs. Hogelman sat at her desk, her hands clasped in front of her. I sat at the desk directly facing hers, where a few minutes before, a girl named Marleen Timmerman had been sitting. The chair was still warm, and the air around me smelled like the grape bubblegum Marleen must have been chewing.

"Oh," I said, and tried to swallow, though my throat was too dry.

"You seemed to be a million miles away in class today. What is it, Eliza? Are you . . . ill? You just, uh . . . don't look right to me, and you're dressed quite warmly for such a hot day. Perhaps you're coming down with something."

She was staring sympathetically at my sweater.

Relieved beyond belief that she was worried about me and not about to kill me, I jumped to my feet and shoved up the sleeves of my sweater.

"No, see, Mrs. Hogelman!" I flung my arms across her desk and turned them over and over to show her my scratches. "I'm fine! I'm just giving myself a beauty makeover, that's all! But thanks for being worried. Can I turn my paper in tomorrow?"

"Uh," she said, then closed her mouth, took off her glasses and rubbed her forehead. "Uh, oh, yes. Of course, Eliza."

◆ ◆ ◆

Talking to Mrs. Hogelman and then running into the rest room to cool my arms made me miss the bus. I called Mama at Skeeter's to ask her what to do.

"Well, hon, I can borrow Roger's car and drive in to pick you up, but it'll be an hour or so before I can leave," she said over the phone. "I can't get away till the afternoon rush is past."

She'd explained to me before that the afternoon rush

was when farmers came into Skeeter's to drink beer and grumble about crop prices before driving their trucks and tractors on home to dinner.

Mama's familiar, comforting voice made things inside me sort of collapse completely, and I could feel tears burning their way up from my throat to my eyes. I sagged against the wall and scratched furiously through my sweater at my arms, since no one was left in the hallway to see.

"Eliza?" Mama asked. "You still there, hon?"

"Yeah," I pushed out. "Pick me up by the public library, okay? I've got homework to do."

Even though this had been a long and miserable day, I still had that stupid how-to paper to write.

CHAPTER
—14—

The library was two blocks from the school, and by the time I got there, sweat was making my arms itch and sting too much for my brain to work. I quickly dropped my books on one of the long oak tables near the encyclopedias. I figured I'd find the rest rooms, cool my arms, then look up pottery, which would make as good a how-to report as anything else I could think of.

The two big ceiling fans seemed to be just pushing sticky globs of air around. I was about to go crazy from that itchy, damp sweater, and I looked around to see if I could safely take it off.

I could see only eight people in the library, counting me.

Two college-looking boys were using the microfiche machine. One had on a University of Missouri T-shirt. "Go Tigers!" it said, and a ferocious animal seemed to jump right out of the boy's back and through that black shirt, all green eyes and sharp teeth.

Three grandmotherly ladies had pulled their leather

chairs into a circle in the periodical section, and were jabbering away in excited whispers about some gardening magazines they were passing around. If they'd been kids, the librarian, Miss Coates, would have lowered the boom on them for sure.

But Miss Coates was sitting on the high wooden stool behind the check-out counter, her chin in her hands and her glasses dangling from a cord around her neck. She pretended she didn't even hear the gardening ladies.

A boy named Rodney Galenberg, who was in a couple of my classes, sat across the library from my table, slouched so far down in a straight-backed chair that he was practically sitting on his neck. He held a book and he looked like what he was reading had him shocked or confused or something. His eyebrows, which met in the middle during the best of circumstances, were in a wild, frowning tangle over his eyes.

I decided nobody that mattered was around to see, and took off my sweater, but I'd just finished hanging it on the back of my chair when a flash of something bright and shiny caught my eye. Someone else was moving through the bookshelves in the research section, not far from me.

Someway, I think I must have almost known who it was before I even saw her, because I quickly fumbled back into my damp sweater.

"Pssst! Liza!"

I jerked my head up. Amanda had just come from behind the encyclopedia shelf like the sun bursting from behind dark clouds, and was leaning in my direction. The two college boys glanced at her, then glanced at each other, whispered something, and laughed a muffled, library laugh. I looked quickly behind my back, then toward her again, and pointed to my chest.

"Me?" I mouthed. I couldn't believe it—she actually knew my name! Amanda Chesselmyer remembered my name and wanted me for something!

"Yes, you, Lisa!" she mouthed back. "Come here! Quick!"

Under my finger my heart flopped like a fish. "Me?" I mouthed again. I couldn't believe this!

"Yes, you, Lisa! Hustle!" Amanda rolled her eyes, and jerked one shoulder toward Miss Coates to warn me to come quickly and quietly.

My chair screeched embarrassingly when I pushed it back. Stupid! I thought, and my face burned as I stood and hurried to Amanda. When I got close she grabbed my arm above the elbow and pulled me far into the narrow, shadowy aisle between the two tall shelves of research books. She stopped when we were out of Miss Coates's range of vision.

"Oh, Liza, you've got to help me!" she whispered, looking imploringly into my eyes.

She'd called me Liza that time, but Lisa two of the four times she'd used my name. Fifty-fifty was wonderful, though, when you thought about it, for someone as popular as she was.

"I haven't had a minute to think about my science project!" she went on in a rush. "You know how it is."

She looked at her hand, then raised it and frowned closely at the nail polish on her thumb.

"Yes," I pushed out, though my lips felt numb. I'd certainly imagined her wonderful busy life plenty of times lately.

My stomach growled, really loud. I was so mortified I felt like I wanted to just die then and there. I cleared my throat and coughed several times to cover up the noise.

Amanda smiled, and smacked the gum she was chewing.

"Listen, you'll be a friend and help me, won't you? With my science project? I think I'm like going to do some research on the ozone layer and stuff. I need this 'O' encyclopedia here to copy some junk out of in my spare time at home."

"You can't check those out," I said, surprised she didn't know that but thrilled that I could help. "You can only use them here, in the library."

"Yeah, right," she said, again, smiling the kind of smile that she and Casey and Lauren used a lot, sort of a tilted smile, just one side of their mouths, with their eyes half shut. On them it looked so cool, but on anybody else it would have looked stupid. "Hey, Lisa, you cut your hair, right? I, like, think it looks really good. I meant to tell you that right off."

I felt so relieved my knees went sort of weak.

"Really?" I asked, in sort of a squeaky whisper.

"May I help you girls?" Miss Coates suddenly stood in

the entrance to the aisle, her mouth pursed up. Amanda turned to her.

"No, but thanks very much," she said, smiling another kind of smile that she and Casey and Lauren used—this one totally open and dazzling and, I don't know, innocent I guess you'd call it. Miss Coates actually smiled back.

When Miss Coates turned to go back to the check-out desk, Amanda dropped her smile immediately. "May I help you, girls?" she mimicked soundlessly toward Miss Coates's back, contorting her face into a hilarious model of Miss Coates's own, then sticking out her tongue.

I tried to quietly but enthusiastically laugh at her joke, so she'd know how flattered I was that she'd gone to the trouble to be entertaining just for me. And I was still reeling from the compliment she'd given me! Evidently Nancy and those cheap-hairspray eighth-grade girls in the rest room and even my mother were fashion amateurs who just couldn't judge these things!

Amanda suddenly grabbed my arm again and leaned close to my ear, serious.

"We better not take any chances," she whispered quickly. "I'll go over to the water fountain and distract her. When the coast is clear, you bring this out to the parking lot, through the back door. I'll meet you out there."

She grabbed the "O" encyclopedia off the shelf and stood listening, not even smacking her gum. Then in one smooth movement she thrust the encyclopedia under the front of my sweater.

"Button it up the rest of the way, and cross your arms," she said, hissing the words under her breath.

And then she was gone, out the bright entrance of the aisle.

I leaned back against the high shelves of reference books, staring at my rectangular front. I couldn't think or breathe or anything. I felt like I'd just slammed into something huge and hard.

From the direction of the water fountain I heard a big commotion—choking, gasping, coughing. Miss Coates's stool moved back with a squeak, and I heard her pointy heels hurrying across the tile floor.

I really had no choice. Everybody knew you didn't just say no to things people like Amanda told you to do, and she'd be mad if I didn't hurry. I squeezed shut my eyes, buttoned my three top buttons, hunched forward my shoulders, and hurried toward the back door, clutching my front like I had the world's worst stomachache. I caught myself and slowed down, but I was pretty sure Miss Coates's eyes were on Amanda, not me.

"Oh, I think my gum is caught in my esophagus!" Amanda was whining from the corner. "Oh, oh, oh! It *hurts!*"

"Now calm down, try to calm down!" That was Miss Coates's high, excited voice. "This has happened to you a couple of other times, remember? Just let me give you

114

a thump or two on the back and then take a little more water and it should go right on down."

Hot air slapped my face as I pushed through the glass double doors at the back of the room. I fumbled down the five concrete stairs and into the parking lot. I ran back to the far corner and collapsed against a car, my legs shaking.

A few minutes later Amanda came out the front door and began nonchalantly scanning the parking lot. She finally spotted me and came striding over, still smacking the gum I guess she'd managed not to swallow. When she got close she held out her hand.

"Good," she said, when I handed her the book. "Hey, thanks, okay? This is cool."

"You'll . . . take it back tomorrow, won't you?" I asked, hoping my voice sounded normal, since I was having trouble breathing exactly right.

"Of course, silly. Hey, what do you think? I'm no thief or anything." She laughed. "Listen, this is definitely cool, Lisa. Definitely."

She walked quickly away then, toward Richview Heights, the fancy suburb I could see in the distance every morning as the bus reached the edge of Pertle Creek.

"Liza," I whispered when I knew she was too far away to hear me correcting her. "Eliza."

CHAPTER
~15~

It seemed like I'd spent hours back in that parking lot, hunched against that car, waiting for Mama. My heart kept beating so hard it felt like I was having a heart attack. In a way, I almost wished I would have a heart attack. Not a fatal one, but the milder kind where they take you to a hospital and you get to lie around and watch TV and everybody makes all the decisions for you.

After a while I realized my books and purse were still in the library, but of course, there was no way I could go back inside to get them. In fact I didn't see how I could ever go inside the library again.

Finally Mama arrived in Skeeter's little green Volkswagen.

"Well, sweetie, how was your day?" she asked as we started out of Pertle Creek. "And what's with the sweater?"

"Fine, and I'm cold," I told her. I turned my face toward the window, hoping she'd leave it at that.

But I could feel her eyes on me, and a few seconds later

she jerked the car back onto the road in the nick of time. We'd been heading for the ditch like a big green turtle hurrying back home.

After that, I think she kept her eyes on the road, but she was too quiet, obviously worrying.

"Eliza, honey, I just don't understand why you cut your hair," she said in a sad voice when we were most of the way home. "That sweater, your hair, how you're acting right now just staring out that window like that—honey, I just don't understand any of this one tiny little bit."

♦ ♦ ♦

We had leftover spaghetti for supper but it felt like worms in my mouth. I was relieved when Hannah came over to talk to Mama, because I needed to be alone to do some hard thinking.

In the privacy of my room I wadded up my pillow, shoved it under my chin, and lay staring at the crystals.

One time Mr. Amos told me that a group of snakes will sometimes tangle themselves into a ball. That's what my brain had felt like since Amanda'd shoved that book under my sweater—a big, twisting snake-ball.

I just needed to sort things out.

First, I was a thief. I couldn't believe it. I was a thief.

Yes, but on the other hand, Amanda was taking the book back tomorrow, before anyone could possibly need it. So maybe I was more of just a borrower. Or maybe, at the very worst, a sort of borrower-thief.

Maybe Amanda had just been using me, even though

she'd used the word 'friend.' "You'll be a friend," she'd said, just exactly like that. "You'll be a friend."

I rose up on my elbows and began rubbing my sore arms. After all, out of seventy-two people in seventh grade, Amanda had chosen me to help her. Me and only me. And I'd read about stuff like this—friendship tests. College sororities did it all the time, made people do hard and sneaky stuff to prove their loyalty. Yes! I rubbed my arms faster. It all made such perfect sense! I was new, and it was the ideal time for her to audition me, right off the bat, before I linked up with other people.

And she'd noticed my hair. She'd liked my hair! My makeover had been the trigger that told her I was probably her, their, kind of cool and potentially (after the scratches healed) pretty person!

"You are so cool, Liza," I whispered, trying to remember Amanda's exact words as she'd walked from the parking lot. "Eliza, you're cool. Li, you are just so cool."

I felt nearly sick to my stomach with happy relief.

"Who are you talking to, Eliza? Yourself?"

I jumped and nearly knocked over one of the crystal jars as Dierdre's face suddenly smashed itself into my screen. "Dierdre, quit sneaking around like that! This window is not your own private doorway!"

She took a step backward, looking confused. "What do you mean? I wasn't trying to climb in your window. It's too far off the ground and the screen is in the way."

I rolled my eyes. "What do you want, anyway?" I mumbled.

"I came to see how your crystals are doing. And to see if you want to come with me to the cave. Tonight I'll start installing the cabin on the raft."

"I'll pass," I muttered. Then I thought of something. "Dierdre, listen! I need a favor. I accidentally left my purse and some books in the public library this afternoon. Could you run over and get them for me during lunch hour tomorrow?"

"Why can't you get them?" she asked.

I thought fast and came up with the perfect answer for her science-book mind. "Well, as you can see, my sapphire crystal is a washout—it hasn't started growing at all. I need to go to the science room at noon to catch Mr. Thurber and ask if there's something I can do to make it work better."

"Good idea," she said immediately. "Sure, I'll get your stuff."

"Thanks. And, uh, I'd go with you tonight, but I have to write that how-to paper for Mrs. Hogelman."

"Oh, right," she said. "See you in the morning."

I watched her walk through the yard, boylike, swinging the ax and the book wide with each step. Then I slid off the bed and went into the bathroom to finger-comb my hair, since I no longer had a brush. It was in my purse, back at the library. I looked at my arms. The scratches looked red and mean, and hurt now more than they itched. Still, it was worth it for the chance it had given me to audition for being Amanda's friend.

◆ ◆ ◆

119

"Your mother is going to bid on Tucker's Grocery tomorrow night," Dierdre informed me on the bus the next morning.

"What are you talking about?" I leaned across her to check my hair in the mirror the window made.

"Your mother told my mother that she's dreamed all her life of running a little store, and that if Tucker's goes cheap enough at B.J. Turley's auction, she's going to buy it. My dad said it's going to be auctioned off this week, remember?"

I snorted a laugh. The first part of what Dierdre just told me was true—Mama, all her life, had dreamed of being a storekeeper. As long as I could remember, she'd had garage sales every time she could talk me into helping her. And sometimes when we came home from grocery shopping she trapped me into playing store with her while we put away the groceries.

"Let's just pretend we're stocking the shelves behind the cash register," she'd say. "Put all the canned fruit together so customers will find it easy. And turn the date stamp outwards when you stick the milk in the fridge. Customers like to know our dairy products are fresh."

But the second thing Dierdre had said, about Mama actually buying a store, was ridiculous. Mama was always talking about things like that in a daydreamy way, but anyone who really knew her didn't take it seriously. She was broke, and that was that.

I began pulling on the sides of my hair to even them up better. "Dierdre, even if she had the money, which she doesn't, why would she pick here to buy a store? She'd pick Kansas City, or maybe Pertle Creek. Dumb old Gouge Eye isn't exactly the center of the universe, you know."

"I know that, Eliza," Dierdre said, and the tone of her voice made me realize I might have hurt her feelings, since this was her hometown and everything.

Charlie was driving past Heckleman's Lumberteria just then, so I made another attempt to get through to her.

"Okay, Dierdre, I'm sorry I called Gouge Eye dumb, but see those rusty orange pig feeders stacked by the For Sale sign at Heckleman's?"

"Of course I see them," Dierdre said snootily, staring straight ahead.

"Well, stop and think. When this town has been gone for a thousand years, some archaeologist will probably be digging around here and those will be the only things he'll find. Those stupid iron pig feeders are the only things in this whole place that matter enough to anybody to be built to last. The archaeologist will think they're our gods, or something. Our idols. You and me and everybody else will be gone, and we'll be thought of as pig worshippers, Dierdre! Doesn't that scare you?"

She turned and looked at me. "Not pig worshippers," she corrected. "Pig *feeder* worshippers."

"See there, Dierdre?" I exploded. "Listen to yourself! Listen to yourself! You sound just like a science book! Your habit of thinking like a book makes you miss the whole point of what's going on around you!"

Her eyes suddenly looked red-rimmed, but her jawline was hard and stubborn so I tried to ignore the fact that her feelings were evidently more hurt than ever. I had better things to do at the moment than to carry on this pointless conversation anyway. I leaned back toward the window to work some more with my hair.

CHAPTER

~16~

Dierdre was nowhere around when I got to the lunch line that day. Nancy said she'd gone to the library to pick up my books and purse, which was what I'd figured. Even though we'd sort of argued on the bus, she had too much of a science-book mind to deviate even slightly from a plan.

Casey and Lauren and Amanda were sitting with some boys at the popular table. Amanda suddenly looked right at me, then leaned across the table to whisper something to Lauren. I shuffled quickly back a couple of feet in line, so it wouldn't look like I was with Nancy. Then Lauren turned to stare right at me too, and actually smiled.

I held my breath—had Amanda just told Lauren how I'd passed the friendship test?

Summoning all my courage, I slightly waved toward them, making it look like I might just be waving at the table beyond them if they didn't respond. But to my amazement, Amanda smiled back, and actually crooked one index finger to tell me to come over!

I snatched up milk and a straw, and went toward them. Nancy said something, but I didn't turn around to hear what it was.

"Is anybody, uh, sitting here?" I asked as calmly as I could when I got near the popular table.

Casey looked at the tiny square of vacant bench beside her, then looked at Lauren, then looked at me.

"I don't see anybody, do you guys?" she said, and Lauren giggled. Amanda snorted and choked on her milk. I sat down as carefully as I could, trying not to look like a klutz—the space was a little smaller than my bottom and I had my hands full of lunch stuff.

"So that party at Twyla's was just so gross," Casey was saying. "You guys were lucky to be out of town. My mom just made me go, and the only good thing was her pool."

"Yeah, their pool's good," Lauren said. "But she has stupid clothes, and wants to show them to you over and over again. Her mom picks them out, even though Twyla's in ninth grade."

Again Amanda laughed.

"Let's go," said Casey. "My hair's ratty."

They all got up and picked up their trays. I was just opening my milk and had only eaten one bite of my sandwich, but quickly followed them, not wanting to be left alone there with just the boys.

They walked bunched-up to the rest room, so I stuck close to them and went in too. When we faced ourselves in the long mirror over the sinks, it seemed to me like

Lauren and Casey were staring at my hair, but Amanda's eyes locked on to mine.

"So, Lisa, I want to tell you thanks again for helping me out yesterday," she said. "I was telling Lauren about it because, like, she hasn't had a chance to start thinking about her science project either."

"I guess you guys are really busy," I said, and smiled.

"Yeah, really," Lauren said with a sigh. "There's stuff all the time."

◆ ◆ ◆

When we left the rest room I glanced down the hall and saw Dierdre leaning against my locker. My purse was over one of her shoulders, and a pile of other stuff was by her feet.

Lauren and Casey and Amanda moved a little way down the hall in the opposite direction.

"Bye, you guys. See you later," I called toward them, but I guessed they didn't hear me because they didn't turn around.

Dierdre was frowning at me when I turned back in her direction to walk toward my locker.

"What?" I said, as I came up beside her and started working the combination of my lock. "Why are you giving me that weird look?"

She shrugged my purse off so it hit the floor with a soft thud.

"So, what did Mr. Thurber have to say about your sapphire crystal?" she asked.

"Mr. Thurber?" I asked, feeling annoyed. Her question not only made no sense, but it made me lose my concentration, and I had to start my combination over.

"That's what I thought," she said. She picked up the books that were lying by her feet, shoved them at me so hard they felt like a kick in the stomach, and started on down the hall toward her class.

"And don't bother to thank me, Eliza. Just don't bother, okay?" she yelled back at me.

Just then something blocked the dim, soupy light coming in through the door at the end of the hall. I turned to see Rodney Galenberg towering over me, his eyebrows moving up and down in excitement.

"I saw you," he said. "At the library."

I swallowed, my face burning. "When?"

"Yesterday," he said. "I saw you take that book."

"But . . . but I . . . I . . ."

"I saw you," he repeated, then turned and walked away, his toes pointed outward, his steps long and slow and serious. He walked exactly like you see those guys walk in old Western movies, those sheriffs that are taking somebody to the gallows, some cowboy gunslinger or somebody.

♦ ♦ ♦

It was awful on the bus going home.

I needed to worry about Rodney Galenberg. If he told Miss Coates or one of the teachers what he had seen, I could be in the biggest trouble of my life.

But I couldn't worry about Rodney because I had to worry about Dierdre first. Silent, poisonous anger had been coming off her in waves through both of the afternoon classes we had together.

And now here we were, sharing a bus seat, mere inches apart.

"Dierdre, I sort of just forgot about going to talk to Mr. Thurber, and I looked all over the cafeteria for you at lunch, even though you always sit by Nancy and I hate sitting by her. She's rude and looks disgusting when she snorts her milk."

I focused my eyes straight ahead as I talked. Somebody had scratched his name—TYLER—into the metal back of the seat in front of us.

I felt Dierdre slowly turn her head to look at me, but I just stared harder at Tyler's name. When had he sat here, in this seat? Last year, five years ago? Was stuff as complicated then as now? Probably not. It probably got a tiny bit more complicated every single day.

"Nancy says you sat by Lauren and those guys at lunch," Dierdre said. "Are you going to sit by them tomorrow, too?"

I jerked my knees up against the seat back and slouched down. "Dierdre, I keep trying and trying to tell you that life is complicated in junior high. How could I possibly know what will happen clear tomorrow?" I stared even harder at Tyler's name, so hard the tail of the "y" seemed to wiggle like a snake. "If they invite me again like they

127

invited me today, it would actually be pretty rude not to. Civilized people don't just turn down lunch invitations for no reason, I mean."

Dierdre didn't say anything else, and neither did I. After a couple of minutes I looked toward her out the corners of my eyes.

She'd had an orange in her hand ever since we'd gotten onto the bus. She was still clenching it, unpeeled. I watched her hand get limper and limper as she sat like a statue, staring straight ahead. Finally, the orange slipped out of her hand, rolled off her lap to the floor, and rolled toward the back of the bus. She didn't even seem to notice it was gone, just sat there with her hand in a limp orange shape.

"We got your orange and we're gonna spit on it!" Jay Roy squealed.

Then Jay Roy, Timmy, and Max, all sounding delirious with joy, began chanting, "We got your orange and we're gonna spit on it! We got your orange and we're gonna . . ."

"Grow up and shut up, you gross little delinquents!" I screamed back at them. "Just spit your stupid little heads off and see what we care!"

I turned back around in my seat, shaking all over. Dierdre didn't even turn my way, but I saw Charlie giving me a shocked look in his rearview mirror.

I spent the rest of the trip staring at Tyler's name again, which seemed to be the only safe thing to pay attention to on the entire bus.

CHAPTER
~17~

When Charlie pulled the bus to our curb, Dierdre's father was throwing stuff from their garage into the back of his pickup.

"Goin' fishin', Rick?" Charlie yelled over our heads. "Gotcha good weather for it, I reckon."

"Yeah, fishin'," Dierdre's father called to Charlie, then flicked his cigarette onto the street and waved in a friendly, carefree way that seemed fakey. I'd never once seen Dierdre's father friendly or the slightest bit carefree.

Charlie swung the door closed and drove on, and Dierdre's father began glowering again. I almost pointed out to Dierdre, before I remembered we weren't speaking, that I couldn't see any fishing gear in the back of the truck. Instead I saw power tools, a portable TV, a bunch of shirts and jeans and boots crammed into a broken plastic laundry basket, and an army-surplus sleeping bag with cotton stuffing sticking out of it in several places like gigantic kernels of popcorn. There were also lots of boxes of small junk, but definitely no fishing rods or bait buckets.

Dierdre spent the same few seconds that I did gawking at the stuff in the truck, then she suddenly hurled her bookbag at the stack of logs. It fell open and spilled her books on the ground. I was shocked—I'd never seen her do anything that unplanned and violent. Especially not to textbooks! I looked up and saw her charging full-speed through the vacant lot across the street.

I slunk quickly toward the trailer, but Rick yelled to me right before I reached it. "Hey, where'd Dierdre run off to?"

"Oh, you know how she likes to hang out at the creek!" I smiled cheerfully, then bolted up the stairs, fell into the kitchen, slammed the door behind me and leaned against it.

"Where's Hannah?" I whispered, my heart racing.

"Well, I don't know, hon." Mama didn't look up from where she sat bent over something on the table. "Oh, I think this was the day she said she'd be cooking for a funeral dinner over at the church all afternoon. Why?"

I noticed then that Mama had four shiny orange cards and was moving them around, making different designs with them, frowning.

She looked up at me. "Why'd you ask about Hannah?"

"Never mind," I said. "What are those things?" I slid into a chair and picked up one of Mama's bright cards. "Tickets?"

"The Heartbreakers are playing the Crystal Palace Saturday night," she said quietly, making the three tickets into a triangle. She plucked the one I held from my hand and put it carefully in the middle. "Burl sent these expensive front-row tickets to us, along with a short note. He said to bring Hannah and Dierdre. We'd be his . . . guests."

I was speechless. Burl, playing the Crystal Palace? Burl, on the same stage with Clint Black and Reba McEntire and people like that? How could this have happened? Burl?

"Well, what do you know about that?" I whispered. "The hair and the clothes and the van did the trick. I've been thinking more and more lately that I've sort of been wrong about Burl. I guess he knows what he's talking about, and image is everything, just like he . . ."

I stopped in midsentence because Mama had stacked up those expensive tickets and was carefully tearing them, first in half, then in quarters, then in eighths. "Rats," she said, when the pieces were too fat for her to tear again. She picked up a double handful of orange confetti, walked to the trash can under the sink, and dropped those scraps into it like shiny, burning snow.

"That man has his nerve, asking me to be his guest," she said, slapping her hands together several times even though it was clear all the ticket pieces were gone from them. "How can I be Burl's guest, Eliza? I'm lots of things to him, or have tried my hardest to be, but a 'guest' just isn't one of them."

"Still, Mama, you have to admit that Burl saw what he

wanted and went after it," I told her. "You just have to admire his . . ."

"I'm going to work," she interrupted, and tromped past me. She slammed the heavy door behind her so hard it blew the remaining ticket shreds off the table and onto the floor.

◆ ◆ ◆

An hour or so later, I heard Rick finally leave in his mysteriously loaded pickup, so I went back out and rescued Dierdre's books. I wiped off the sawdust and dead grass, loaded them neatly into her bookbag, brought it to her porch and left it on the swing for her. I thought about waiting there, too, but lost my nerve. I couldn't figure out if I was scared of Rick returning, or of having to think of something to say to Dierdre.

I went inside, took a bath, washed my hair and fiddled with it for a while, ate some of the meatloaf Mama had made, rotated my crystals, then went on to bed because I wanted to get up early. I wanted time to catch the bus two blocks down, where it stopped in front of the bait shop to pick up Janelle Ferguson. That way, I'd be in our seat, and Dierdre would be the one to have to decide whether we were going to sit together, or whether we were too mad.

◆ ◆ ◆

I woke just as the sun rose over the frizzy weed field behind the trailer. As I stretched and got my eyes completely open, I watched the pinkish-yellow dawn light hitting my crystal jars and covering the ceiling with patterns. There were dancing prisms from the eight fast-growing alums, and rich patterns of red from the three tiny but gorgeous rubies. At first I thought I saw something else, some faint hint of blue toward one corner.

I quickly sat up and looked closely at the sapphire jar, but all I could see was a little gross-looking, crusty stuff along its string. The sapphire was a complete dud. The blue on the ceiling was either a shadow or a spider web.

I scratched at my arms and let my mind carefully go over the events in the cafeteria yesterday. I had eaten lunch at the popular table. Me, Eliza Marie Branniman. If I'd been someone looking our way I would have envied me as I myself had envied each of those girls in Winstead's just a couple of weeks ago.

I knew it was dangerous to attach too much significance to one lunch, but it was hard not to, since it had come right after the friendship audition in the library.

"I saw you take that book." The unwelcome memory of Rodney's voice immediately butted in at the thought of the library.

I looked down at my arms. The red lines seemed to be slightly fading, but teensy dark hairs were growing again all over the place. My hair looked fairly swingy since I'd washed it, though.

◆ ◆ ◆

When Dierdre got on the bus, she sat in a seat by herself.

In fact, she totally ignored me in all our morning classes.

Since she was acting so snooty, I wasn't especially surprised when she didn't come into the cafeteria at lunch. I figured she'd taken her lunch sack out to some isolated corner of the schoolyard where she could enjoy the uninterrupted company of that fat book of hers. Nancy and a bunch of other girls were sitting at her table, talking and laughing. When I had my milk and napkin collected, I took a deep breath and glanced carefully toward the popular table. Lauren caught my eye and waggled her fingers, gesturing wildly for me to join them.

"Got any ideas for my science project yet?" she asked eagerly as I came close.

I guess partly because my mind was still on Dierdre being gone, the question took me by surprise. "Ideas?" I croaked out, then immediately hoped I hadn't sounded stupid.

"You know!" Lauren said, pulling her hair back, then fluffing it with her fingers and letting it go. "Amanda told you yesterday! I can't get a start on it."

"Oh," I said. "Right!"

I couldn't see any real place to sit, though there was almost room right on the edge of the bench if I used my left leg to brace myself. I slid in there, and hoped I looked relaxed and cool with my leg rigid that way.

"Lisa, listen," Amanda said, leaning toward me across the table. "We help each other, see? Like, Casey knows make-up stuff, and gives us facials."

They all three looked at me.

"I could give you one sometime," Casey said.

"Thanks," I answered.

"And I meant to tell you. I'm having a party in maybe two or three weeks and you're definitely invited," Amanda added.

"Really?" I'm sure that word came out squeaky and I sounded totally uncool. A party in Richview Heights—this was the kind of thing I'd always dreamed about!

"So since you're smart, Lauren needs this help with her science project," Amanda repeated. "Today's the day we have to tell Mr. Thurber what we're doing, remember?"

They were all staring at me, leaning forward on their elbows, waiting, so I tried to concentrate.

"Uh, well, you could do a crystal-growing project," I heard myself tell Lauren. "You could grow rubies and . . . and sapphires. I could get the stuff for you and start you out, okay?"

She shrugged, and looked at the others. They shrugged back, but Casey opened her eyes a little wider.

"Bring it Monday?" Lauren said.

"Sure." I cracked my face into a smile. "Fine."

They stood up to go then, and I quickly collected my half-eaten lunch to follow them to the rest room.

♦ ♦ ♦

Dierdre sat alone again on the bus going home. She sat where she had that morning, near the obnoxious boys in the back. Several times I was sure I felt her eyes cutting two laser holes between my shoulder blades, but each time I whirled around she was looking out the window.

♦ ♦ ♦

135

That afternoon I sat staring at the crystals, trying to figure out how to transport them to school on Monday. And how would I get sapphires? Could I possibly take paint or something and color the plasticky alums blue? Also, what was I going to do for *my* science project? Mr. Thurber had already docked 5 percent from the grade of everyone who didn't turn in a project idea today. And Monday it would be another 5 percent!

Mama got home early from Skeeter's and peeked around the edge of my doorway. "Knock, knock," she called. "What you up to in here by your lonesome?"

"Nothing," I said, reaching frantically for my sweater.

"Don't bother with that." She bounced down to sit beside me on my bed. "I saw your arms last night when I came to check on you in your sleep. Itchy?"

"A little," I admitted, and to my surprise she laughed softly as she slipped an arm around my shoulders.

"You know what? When I was eleven years old my cousin Dotty and I decided to shave our eyebrows off. It was the style then to have thin little eyebrows, and we thought we should just shave our big old overgrown ones off and draw on little teensy ones. She drew hers with a brown Magic Marker, but orange was the only marker at all close to my hair color. If we didn't look like a couple of clowns, especially me with those two bright and shiny orange squiggles in the middle of my face! People laughed and laughed, especially the boys. My, what we gals will go through for so-called beauty, huh?"

"You're already beautiful," I whispered, leaning

against her a little. My eyes felt hot. "So you don't have to worry."

She bent her elbow to pull my head close and whispered in my ear, "I know you won't believe this, but neither do you."

She pulled me into a hug and we just stayed that way for a while. I closed my eyes and listened to the outside sounds—kids yelling from their bikes, dogs barking along behind them, birds sounding so cheerful it almost tricked you into thinking the world was just a big, blue, uncomplicated ball.

"Eliza, I'm sorry things have been so crazy this first week of school, what with Burl staying gone and this new job of mine and all," Mama whispered into my hair. "Is there anything you want to talk about, sweetie? Anything at all?"

I shook my head against her, swallowing, and squeezing my eyes shut, hard.

"Okay." She began stroking my hair, rocking us back and forth. "Okay, but just remember, I'm here for you, always."

For a long time we leaned together like that, rocking. Finally she gave me a last squeeze and let me go. "I better rustle us up some grub," she said, her voice a little husky.

But when she reached the doorway, she stopped and leaned back against the wall, looking toward my window. The setting sun was reaching fingerlike beams right through the alums and rubies.

"I would give the world if your dad could see that," she said softly.

◆ ◆ ◆

After dinner I was in my bedroom again, trying once more to come up with a plan for making the crystals good enough for Lauren, when Dierdre's face suddenly smashed itself into my screen.

"I need to talk to you, Eliza," she said, so slowly and solemnly her screen-flattened face looked and sounded like a mask of doom from some weird science-fiction movie. "Right now."

"Oh, yeah, great." I cleared my throat. "If you wanted to talk so bad, why'd you avoid me on the bus and at school all day?"

"I couldn't talk to you about this on the bus. I didn't think you'd want everybody on the bus to know you're a thief. Rodney Galenberg told me what he saw at the library."

CHAPTER
—18—

I couldn't think. I couldn't breathe. I sat there frozen, but on fire. I knew my neck was turning a guilty-looking pink, even though there was a logical explanation that Dierdre didn't know.

"I cannot believe, Dierdre, that you just called me a thief," I said in a low, hurt voice. "I cannot believe you would let a complete stranger make up things about me like that!"

"So Rodney Galenberg . . . lied?" she asked.

"Yes, Dierdre!" I yelled, pounding the bed with my fists. "Yes, yes, yes, okay?"

She stood there for a while. She didn't speak and it was impossible to know what she was thinking, since her face was smashed tight into the screen without room left over for an expression.

Finally she turned, and walked off into the darkness.

I tilted over, and covered my face with my hands, hoping I could start crying instead of thinking. But I couldn't, now that she was gone.

Before too long, though, my brain got exhausted and I fell asleep.

◆ ◆ ◆

I awoke when it was completely dark. I had the feeling it was late, and sure enough, my little digital clock said 10:47. Still, there were voices in the kitchen.

I carefully opened my door a crack.

". . . just never liked fishing before. This is a totally new thing for him, and I've thought about it and thought about it ever since he left last night. I thought about it all last night and I thought about it all day today, and still I just can't decide what to think about it."

That was Hannah.

"Well, men just seem to have to let off steam, you know it? If he said he was going fishing for a few days, all you can do is be glad he's not out tomcattin' around. I think that's what you're gonna just have to think, Hannah. Don't you think?"

That was Mama. She'd probably just gotten home from Skeeter's, and Hannah had seen the kitchen light and come over.

I closed my door and went on to bed for good. The last thing I needed was to have to hear about thinking. It might make me start thinking myself again, and I'd never get back to sleep.

◆ ◆ ◆

Dierdre was in my window again when I woke up Saturday morning. I don't know how long she'd been there. She was looking at the crystals, peering at each one

140

separately with this absorbed look on her face, so she might have been there for a long time.

"Good, you're awake. I need your help," she said when she noticed one of my eyes was the tiniest bit slitted open. "The raft is finished. It'll take two people to get it out of the cave and over to the creek bank."

"Can't you find someone who's not a thief to help you?" I couldn't help asking.

She missed my sarcasm, though, as usual. "No. You're the only person I've told about my raft," she said. "I need you."

♦ ♦ ♦

She said we'd move the raft the same way the Egyptians probably moved those big stone blocks when they built the pyramids. We used three straight, long logs that she'd peeled and smoothed. Grunting, we lifted up the edges of the raft until we'd managed to kick and shove all three logs underneath it. Then I pulled the raft over those three logs with the thick tether rope Dierdre had tied to the front. Each time we left a log behind, Dierdre grabbed it and shoved it back under the front of the raft, so we always had three wheels to skid the raft slowly along.

She had the hard part of the job, but when we finally got the raft to the sandy creek bank, I was exhausted, too.

"Let's shove it on into the water," she said, her eyes wide with excitement as she tied the loose end of the short tether rope securely around a small sycamore tree.

We shoved, and the raft floated a couple of feet from shore like, well, a raft. Actually, with the cabin on top, it could almost have been called a real boat. I had the same thought I'd had that first night I saw her workshop inside the cave—it really was pretty impressive.

I waded into the creek so my back was to Dierdre, and splashed water on my sweaty arms and neck. "Dierdre, listen, about Rodney Galenberg. I didn't mean to imply he was a liar. It's just that what he thought he saw wasn't what he saw at all. I just . . . borrowed a book. An encyclopedia, that is. I mean, I didn't even borrow it. Amanda just asked me to help her borrow it. It was for a good cause, and I'm sure she's returned it by now."

My explanation had sounded really good to me. Tight, accurate, and almost noble or something.

I heard the water splash behind me and turned to see Dierdre standing on the raft, her arms slightly out to the sides for balance and her eyes glistening. She seemed so much in her own world that I doubted if she'd even really heard what I'd been saying.

"Dierdre? Do you understand? About not telling Rodney I said he lied?"

I couldn't afford to make him mad, not with what he knew.

She looked at me. "What good cause?" she asked.

"Huh?"

"What good cause did you have for stealing that encyclopedia? You said it was for a good cause, but don't you figure everybody who does bad stuff thinks they have a good cause? Do you think thieves steal just for the fun of it? Do you think liars lie just for kicks, Eliza?"

"Dierdre, how can you twist everything around like that!" I clomped out of the water and began slip-sliding up the muddy bank. "Didn't you hear anything I just said? It was borrowing, not stealing!"

I was so tired and angry I was shaking all over. Why bother trying to reason with someone like her, someone who looked at everything way too simply, like books made everything seem? She could just stay ignorant, and unpopular, and totally weird all through junior high, for all I cared.

She slowly sat down cross-legged on the raft. "Eliza, you don't have to worry. I'm not going to tell anybody what Rodney told me, and I know he won't tell either. He just told me because he said you and I were like, well, best friends and everything. I mean, he thought that."

"Okay," I said, and swallowed hard. "Thanks."

But my voice sounded stringy, like those two short words had leaked out of me. I turned and began trudging out of the woods. The trees seemed to blur into the hot, light blue sky.

I walked on into those blurry trees and kept on walking, not paying attention to the cockleburrs or the heat or the pounding starting in my brain or much of anything.

When I finally got back to the trailer I grabbed the first box I could find and crammed my messy crystal jars into it, then shoved it under the bed where I didn't have to look at it.

◆　◆　◆

That night was the night B. J. Turley was going to try to auction off the old grocery store building. Mama asked if I wanted to go to the auction with her and Hannah and Dierdre.

"Hannah's worried," she said sadly. "Rick's been gone two days and two nights and, frankly, I don't think she thinks he's fishing. She needs something to get her mind off things, and the auction might do the trick."

"I'll stay here," I said listlessly. Being with Dierdre was too tricky and hard. What if, for instance, she'd seen my empty window this afternoon and started asking me a bunch of brain-strain questions about where the crystals were?

◆ ◆ ◆

But alone in the trailer, I kept smelling those chemicals in the soggy box under my bed, and I found myself staring at the crusty white rings on the windowsill where the jars had been. The only jar left there was the dud sapphire, which I hadn't wanted to pack because Lauren would think it was dumb and ugly.

I folded my arms on the empty windowsill and put my cheek down on my hands. A few grainy chunks of blue were clinging in stupid, helter-skelter directions along the string. I picked up the jar, rotated it slowly, and put it back down. All the chemicals from the bottom swirled desperately around, trying with all their might to get ahold of that string, to become something beautiful.

But minutes later those chemicals settled back on the bottom again, hopeless-looking blue junk, ugly as ever.

144

A tightness started in my throat and began moving into my forehead. Maybe the smell of the boxed-up chemicals was getting into my bloodstream and making me crazy. Or maybe I was like Hannah and needed to get my mind off things. Though, I reminded myself, things were good for me, very good with my new almost-friends and getting invited to a party in Richview Heights and everything.

Still, I just suddenly had to get out of there, so I went to the auction after all.

◆ ◆ ◆

Cars and pickups were parked thick along the street for three blocks on each side of B. J.'s, and the dogs used to sleeping in the road looked irritated at having to move to the gutters. I slunk along the edges of the crowd, picking things up from the long auction tables and putting them down again.

By the time I'd been there about an hour, staying far back in the shadows to avoid Mama and Dierdre and Hannah, it was nearly dark and most of the cars and pickups had disappeared.

"Friends, now don't you go home just yet, because the best is yet to come!" B. J. Turley suddenly announced through the horn-shaped loudspeaker he carried around. He tilted his cowboy hat back a little and wiped his face with his handkerchief, then jumped down off the wagon he'd been standing on. "Right down the street is some prime real estate to be auctioned away right here and now!"

A few people laughed at that, but the crowd shifted like

a many-headed caterpillar to follow B. J. down the block. I watched Mama's bright orange hair glowing in the sunset as she stayed toward the very front of the crowd. Even from half a block behind her, I could tell she was bouncing on her heels in excitement.

B. J. opened the bidding. Two men I didn't know got into a hot and fast bidding war, which seemed to really surprise the Gouge Eye citizens, who moved their heads eagerly back and forth between the two like spectators watching a championship tennis match.

"Them two is both demolition men," I heard a man near me tell his neighbor. "One from Clark's Junction, one from Branson. I reckon they want to tear the place down for the bricks."

When the bidding reached nine hundred dollars, B. J. Turley looked meaningfully from one bidder to another. The Clark's Junction man, after a long time, raised the bid.

"Nine-fifty," he muttered.

I could hardly stand to look at Mama. There had been absolutely no way she could bid on that store, thank goodness. Still, from this distance, she seemed so small and suddenly quiet and . . . defeated.

"Nine-fifty going once," B. J. sang out. "Going twice . . ."

Then in the blink of an eye everything changed.

"B. J., I'll give you eleven hundred dollars cash money for Tucker's store," came a deep, calm voice from clear across the street. "That is, provided Miss Lorna Jean

146

Branniman will consent to direct its renovation for me and will agree to manage it once it's reopened."

Everyone drew in their breath, too shocked to react for a few seconds. Then all of us turned at once and saw Roger, as Mama, and Mama alone, called him, standing outlined in the doorway of his restaurant. He was wearing his usual white T-shirt and white tennis shoes and his jeans and grease-stained apron, chewing on a toothpick with his short, muscular arms crossed.

The two men who'd been bidding looked at each other, then looked at the ground, then shook their heads.

"Suh . . . sold to Mr. Skeeter Skelton for eleven hundred dollars!" B. J. Turley called, scratching the back of his head.

"Yahoo!" Mama yelled. She locked eyes with Skeeter for several seconds and mouthed "thank you" across to him, then she started jumping up and down and punching her fists in the air like a prizefighter. "And while you all are gathered here, I'd like to invite each and every one of you to our grand opening, sometime soon!"

CHAPTER
—◦19◦—

Mama spotted me in the crowd then and waved with both hands as she came rushing toward me. Smiling people parted quickly for her on both sides, like you'd part for a charging bull.

"Y'all come on over and have some ice cream to celebrate," Skeeter called to the crowd, and everyone began laughing and talking and heading in the general direction of the restaurant.

I seemed to be the only person not moving. I stood there frozen to the spot, waiting for Mama as the world spun in an out-of-control way around me.

"Liza, Liza, Liza! We got it, hon!" Mama cried as she reached me. She grabbed me, hugged me hard, then slid one arm around my neck and pulled my head close to her own, whispering, "Well, actually, Roger got it, but I know he wouldn't have done it except that I've been joking around at the restaurant about my dream of running a little grocery store someday. Can you believe that? He's just the sweetest man, Eliza. Just the very sweetest man!"

She jumped up and down a few times, and pulled me limply along. I couldn't get my breath or my brainpower back enough to think, let alone talk, but that didn't seem to worry her.

"Oh, Eliza, isn't it just beautiful?" she said, staring at the building, her voice husky and awed-sounding.

I looked where she was looking, roaming my eyes over the ugly two-story brick building in front of us.

It had once been painted shocking pink, a much more flamboyant pink than the trailer, but most of the paint had flaked away. The big windows in front were broken out, and barn swallows flew back and forth, in and out. Through the shadows I could see that most of the ceiling was lying on the floor in big, plastery pieces.

"This is it, Li," Mama whispered in my ear. "This is just exactly what I've dreamed about all my entire live-long life."

And then she flung her arms out like she was hugging the whole night sky, threw back her head, and began twirling around and around right there in the street. She worked her way toward Skeeter's still twirling like that, laughing and every so often shouting, "My dream has come true, true, true!"

She obviously wasn't talking to me any longer but to herself and maybe the stars. It was a thing I didn't dare interrupt, like a prayer or an important telephone conversation.

When she was nearly to the restaurant I sat down heavily in the road, knowing no cars would come now that the day's big event was over and everyone who was still awake was eating ice cream at Skeeter's.

"We'll be here now until we rot," I said out loud, testing the words. But the idea just wouldn't sink in.

I touched my arm, felt sharp prickles of tiny hairs growing out. The red light on top of the highest elevator tower was blinking in the corner of my eye like a fake ruby crystal. A ruby that would turn out to be dirty, scratched plastic if you got close, say in a low-flying plane.

"We'll be here till we rot!" I said, more forcefully, to the deserted street.

But still the idea wouldn't sink in, and I began to realize I'd had a plan in the back of my mind, a plan to talk Mama into moving to Pertle Creek where normal people lived. Or maybe even to a really cheap outskirt of Richview Heights. Amanda, Lauren, and Casey would seem as out of place in Gouge Eye as diamonds set in a plastic ring from a bubble-gum machine. But now Mama would never give up this so-called store, so I'd be stuck here whether I fit or not.

I took a deep breath, blew it out to clear my brain, and pulled my knees up under my chin and off the sharp gravel. Okay, how much actual damage was this going to do to my relationship with Amanda and Lauren and Casey? At least I'd been careful not to tell anyone at school where I lived. As far as I knew, no one in Pertle Creek had any reason to suspect, yet, that I lived in Gouge Eye. What if I just told everyone that I lived on, maybe, a farm? No, a ranch! That sounded fancier, and since Dierdre and I were the only junior high kids on the bus, how would Amanda and those guys find out the truth? That is, if I could someway get Dierdre to play along, which of course would be a pretty big if.

Where was Dierdre, anyway? I thought of my empty crystal window and jumped to my feet, trying to remember when I'd last seen her. She hadn't been standing with Hannah and Mama during the bidding for the store. She could be snooping around outside the trailer right this second.

Expecting to see her skinny neck craning into my window, I ran toward home, but stopped halfway there, about even with the church. My lungs suddenly burned and I bent double, coughing. I tried to get a deeper breath, choked, and looked up to see what was wrong with the air.

A bright orange tongue was licking at the night sky right over Dierdre's house! I opened my mouth to scream for help, but as I turned back toward town, out of the corner of my eye I saw a shadow slide through the wild raspberry vines that grew along the alley behind the church. I covered my mouth and nose with the tail of my T-shirt and froze in place, peering into the darkness back there. Seconds later, Dierdre's father, crouching low, moved stealthily from the raspberry tangle into the moonlight, then ran on into the deep darkness beyond town.

"Fire!" I screamed then, running flat-out back toward Skeeter's. "Help! Everybody, fire! Fire!"

People came streaming out of the restaurant, running

toward the shed behind the Lumberteria where the volunteer fire department's water tank was kept on a hay wagon. A group of men hurried to a pickup, returned with a huge wrench, and began working to open the hydrant in front of the bait shop.

Hannah came toward me, her eyes dark and glistening, and grabbed my arms above the elbows. "Where's Dierdre?"

"I . . . I don't . . . don't know. I'll find her!" I called over my shoulder as I began running toward the vacant lot.

♦ ♦ ♦

I almost ran right into Dierdre halfway through the soybean field. She was just standing there, cradling her book against her chest, and the fire was reflected in both of her eyes.

I hadn't run very far, but still I was shaking all over and my knees felt ready to buckle.

"Oh, Dierdre! Your mother was so worried! Come on!"

I grabbed her wrist, but she didn't follow along. She just let me hold her limp arm out in the air, like she didn't notice I was doing it.

"He's not coming back this time," she said in a low, flat voice.

It's hard for me to describe how she looked, how I could tell that though she stood there so still and straight and seemed perfectly calm, I knew she was shattering to pieces inside. You probably have to have been in that position yourself to understand. It's like you know no amount of screaming or crying will do any good and so you are just calm beyond calm. It's like your body becomes a shell that has to immediately freeze thick and solid so the pieces that used to be you won't fall completely out of it.

I dropped her wrist and went to stand next to her. I turned and faced in the direction she was facing and we watched her house burn quickly to the ground.

"If he set that fire, he could have been caught in it. That happens sometimes when people set them. I don't even know if he's safe," she whispered hoarsely. "That's the worst part."

I licked my lips. "Dierdre, I . . . I saw your father, running from the fire, through the back alley behind the church, then on out of town. So don't worry. He's safe."

She took a deep breath and closed her eyes like she'd taken a punch, but something about the way she did it told me I'd done the right thing, telling her.

"Come on, okay?" I said gently, taking her wrist again.

This time she went with me toward the smoke, toward the confusion and shouts and the line of bright embers dying along the foundation of what used to be her house.

♦ ♦ ♦

A bunch of people worked in Dierdre's yard till after midnight, manning hoses and passing buckets and slapping at embers with wet gunnysacks from the elevator until every small piece of fire was gone. It was strange in a way—the wood stacked in a ring around the yard got black and sooty but didn't burn.

"Wood that newly cut and green don't burn easy," I

heard one of the men say. "Lucky it was there—probably kept the fire from spreading."

The wind was strong from the east that night and blew most of the smoke way across the fields, so we could sleep in the trailer as long as we kept the windows closed.

Hannah and Mama slept in Burl's room, and Dierdre slept with me. She faced the wall, and I faced the window, where the lone crystal jar picked up the eerie, smoky moonlight and seemed filled with bluish smoke itself.

I kept hearing her muffled sniffling. "Dierdre, he'll be back. Don't worry," I finally said quietly, turning onto my back. "He loves you, and he loves your mom."

"But what's that have to do with it?" she whispered, her voice weak and shaky. "You have to make choices. He chose something that wasn't us. When you go toward one thing you turn your back on something else. That's just how it works."

Something steely cold slid into my heart like a knife when she said that, and I started talking partly to block out the pain.

"When the fireworks factory exploded three years ago, they couldn't call us. If they could have called us I might have seen him one more time. But they couldn't. That was the worst thing."

I put those awful words into the air and then lay there feeling crushed under them, holding my breath in the darkness. Tears began sliding into my ears.

"Why couldn't they call you?" Dierdre whispered.

I tried to breathe carefully, but still it hurt. "Our phone

wasn't working." That cold knife turned and turned. The air crushed down harder and harder. "We didn't have the money that month to pay our bill so they disconnected it. There's always something we don't have the money for, and that month it was the phone."

"So that's what you meant that night in the woods, about unreliable phones," Dierdre whispered. "No wonder you looked like you looked."

I couldn't say another word or think another thought. I turned back onto my side again and tried to pretend I was nothing, just a cloud or a wisp of windy air with no memory, no pain, no fear. That old trick had sometimes worked right after the explosion, back in fourth grade, but it didn't work now. I clenched my teeth as the chunks of gritty blue along the string in the jar spread out like exploding stars. I raised the sheet and squeezed it against my eyes.

"I built the raft . . ." Dierdre whispered slowly. "I mostly built the raft . . ."

And suddenly there was a roaring in my ears, and I knew that no matter what, I had to stop her from finishing that sentence. I was right on the verge of being accepted like I'd never been accepted before, by the kind of girls I wanted to be like more than anything in the world. Girls like the girls in the corner booth at Winstead's. Ruby girls, not dime-a-dozen alums grown in places like rusted-out little Gouge Eye, places where people lived only because the living was cheap. I would be their friend! Not the waitress's daughter, but their real true friend!

"Dierdre, it'll be okay," I blurted. "It'll be okay! You built the raft because you're a true scientist. You can tether it in the current now and get great measurements and you'll have by far the best science project and get the medal at Mr. Thurber's science fair. Things will be all right! Things will seem much, much brighter in daylight, so let's just get some sleep."

I pulled the pillow over my head, and for a long time I lay there, breathlessly listening to the pounding of my own heart.

CHAPTER
—20—

The morning after the fire we went to church with Hannah. I guess she knew the sermon would be directed right at her, and she needed Mama to sit there beside her, handing her tissues, holding her hand. Dierdre and I sat stiffly on either side of them, staring straight ahead of us.

"Any man or woman must say it's a sad and cruel tragedy that has taken the home of our sister Hannah and her family. But as a community of believers we know that neither fire, nor flood, nor, nay, even pestilence will separate us from the love that sustains us through all things, forever and amen!"

"Amen," echoed a few people as Reverend Hartsill stopped for breath. To keep from thinking about Hannah's soft whimpering, I concentrated on the way he'd pronounced the word "cruel." He'd said "crew-el," like it had two syllables.

Hannah sobbed, "Yes, Lord!" I glanced at her out the sides of my eyes. She had borrowed Mama's green silk dress, and since she was so much shorter and pudgier than Mama, the buttons down the front were stretched nearly to the pop-off point, but the material between them sagged open, showing the black slip she'd also borrowed from Mama. It seemed so sad that she had to wear that too-long black slip with that too-tight green dress.

Dierdre was wearing Mama's clothes, too. There was no way anything of mine would have fit her, but Mama's red skirt looked just about right.

Mama picked up one of the cardboard fans with MIS-SOURI FARM ASSOCIATION in huge red letters that the elevator must have donated to the church. She handed it to Dierdre, and Dierdre knew she meant for her to fan Hannah with it, so she did.

♦ ♦ ♦

When church was finally over, everybody crowded around Mama and Hannah on the concrete stairs outside, and Dierdre and I managed to dodge through the crowd and escape. I wasn't surprised when she turned into the vacant lot and went toward the creek instead of directing us back toward the trailer.

"Dierdre, do you think your mother suspects . . . suspects that, you know, your father . . . well, you know."

We'd reached the field, and she snatched a soybean pod and peeled it as she walked.

"I heard her tell your mother that he would be just sick when he came home from fishing and saw what had happened," she said, and threw down the pod. "It hasn't

158

crossed her mind that he snuck back into town when he knew everybody'd be at the auction and set the fire himself."

I sighed. Dierdre's mother and my mother were so much alike. Neither of them could believe anything bad about anybody until it hit them right between the eyes. "We mustn't tell her," Dierdre said quickly. "Okay? Not yet. She couldn't . . . handle it."

"Right, we won't," I agreed, just as quickly.

We walked silently then until we got to the creek, where Dierdre's raft was tied to the sycamore tree and bobbed partway in the water.

"We'll take it out for its first run," she said, hopping lightly onto the raft and crouching to begin untying the tether knots. "Climb aboard."

To tell the truth, I wasn't crazy about doing that. When the last tether knot was loosened from the rudder, you could tell the rope would quickly unwind itself and let the strong current have the raft for a playtoy. Only the spike Dierdre had hammered through the thick knot at the very end of the rope and into one of the back logs of the raft would stop us.

"Hurry," she said, looking up at me. She had dark circles under her eyes, and her movements seemed choppy and nervous. "We won't go far, just twenty yards, then the rope will play out and pull taut and hold us in the rapids."

"*If* the spike at the very end of the rope holds," I said,

stepping gingerly onto the raft. "*If* the rope doesn't break. *If* the knot around the tree doesn't give."

"I've got eight knots around the tree and the spike is hammered a good two inches into that log," she said. "The only way that raft could break free is if I cut the rope with my ax."

I didn't ask any more questions because suddenly she reached the last of the rudder knots and untied it, and it took all my energy to grab hold and hang on for dear life as we shot downstream. Seconds later the rope pulled taut and the raft jerked to a halt in the rapids in the middle of the creek. It yanked violently back and forth sideways a few times like a big, angry dog reaching the end of its leash and trying desperately to keep on running, but the rope held firm against the spike.

Dierdre stood up, grabbed a long pole that was lying between two logs, and leaned against it for balance in the middle of the bucking raft.

"Isn't this wonderful?" she shouted above the noise of rushing water. The wind moved through her short, spiky hair like excited little fingers.

I'd been lying spread-eagled on my stomach, trying to clutch the logs with both my hands and feet, so I carefully turned over and pushed myself up until I managed to sag with my back against the cabin wall.

"Wow," I said, trying to catch my breath. "Oh, wow."

"Yeah," she shouted. "And it must be even more wonderful to drift completely free, just carried along by the current. Twisted Creek runs into the Missouri River, and the Missouri eventually meets the Mississippi. Can you imagine, Eliza? Sailing down the mighty Mississippi without a worry in your head?"

I shut my eyes, felt things spinning, and quickly opened them again. My mouth tasted funny.

"There are really . . . really big rapids beneath . . . beneath the highway bridge at the edge of town," I wheezed, crossing my arms and squeezing my stomach. "You'd smash to pieces and drown before you got two miles downstream. So I guess you could worry about *that.*"

I was thinking that at least if I threw up, I'd throw up in the water.

"Maybe," she said dreamily. "Maybe not." Then, "Neither fire nor flood nor pestilence will stop me now."

"Oh, Dierdre," I shouted up to her. "Why do you have to say dumb-sounding things like that? Sometimes you just sound so . . . so uncool."

She looked down at me. "That's religious, remember? Reverend Hartsill used it in his sermon this morning."

"I know, I know. But religious or not, saying stuff like that isn't good for your image one bit! The way you talk like a science book, or in this case like a Bible or something, well, sometimes, Dierdre, it makes my follicles stand on end."

"Follicles don't stand on end," she said, leaning on that pole and squinting ahead of her, into the glaring, rushing water. She looked so wild-eyed and pale and strange, like a crazy pirate or something. "They're the little holes your

161

hair grows from. The hair itself is what stands on end."

I felt really nauseous by then. "Anything you say, Dierdre," I grumbled, and put my head between my knees. "Just get me off this thing, okay?"

CHAPTER
~21~

Dierdre used the long pole to maneuver us back to the shore, where we wound the tether rope back around the rudder and secured the raft again by the sycamore tree.

She stayed crouched beside the creek for a long time, staring into the water and tearing up leaves.

"So what's your plan?" I finally asked impatiently. "You're planning to float out into the current like that every day, right, to take wind and current measurements for your science project?"

"Yeah," she said listlessly as she dropped a handful of leaves and stood up. "And depth readings."

She turned and started slowly climbing the bank, moving stiffly, like a sleepwalker.

"Your plans sound wonderful," I said as I followed her. "Mr. Thurber will definitely, definitely be impressed."

But still, in spite of how I was bending over backward to be nice, she just slouched broodily along.

"Okay, what's wrong?" I finally asked, sighing elaborately. "You're still mad about that follicle thing, right?"

"Follicle thing?" she said softly. She stopped walking, but didn't turn to face me. "What are you talking about?"

I came up right behind her then, where she stood stock-still looking straight ahead. I stood on tiptoe and looked over her shoulder. Directly in front of us the last bars of shade rippled across the trail, and the woods ended. In the distance Gouge Eye shimmered in the heat, without her house in its usual spot. Her scorched yard was a horrible empty place in the row of houses, like a missing tooth in the middle of a smile. And I knew she was seeing an even bigger and more horrible empty space, another, bigger thing vanished into thin air. She was definitely thinking of her father.

"Dierdre, listen, I forgot for a second about last night. I mean, I'm . . ."

But the rest of my apology stuck in my throat. In fact I suddenly got the same feeling I'd had the night before when I'd pulled my pillow over my head, the roaring-in-my-ears feeling.

How could I tell her how sorry and sad I was for her without sounding like Rodney had been right about that best-friend thing?

As I hesitated, I felt her stiffen, as though with real fear.

"Oh, no, is that a fire truck?" she whispered. "Do you . . . do you think the county fire marshal is here to investigate? Do you think they . . . suspect something?"

I shaded my eyes with my hand and squinted into the distance. A big cherry-red vehicle was just pulling up in front of the trailer and the lot where Dierdre's house had been.

"What's *Burl* doing here?" I shouted, and began running.

◆ ◆ ◆

The kitchen of the trailer smelled like a bakery when we burst in, and the counters were filled with pans and foil-wrapped dishes. Several teetering stacks of cardboard boxes and bulging brown paper sacks took up most of the floor space. Dierdre and I edged in beside the refrigerator.

Mama and Hannah were seated at the kitchen table, like two dolls crammed into an overflowing toy box.

"Oh, girls, would you just look at all this?" Hannah cried out to us, dabbing her eyes with a tissue. "Everyone in town has stopped by, bringing food and clothes. Everyone has been so . . . so wonderful." She reached forward and grabbed Dierdre's wrist. "Honey, you didn't run into your dad fishing anywhere out there, did you?"

"No," Dierdre said, and I felt her wince.

"Where's Burl?" I demanded, partly to change the subject.

Mama frowned, bit her bottom lip and took a deep breath. "Well, girls, he just went in to take a little nap. Seems the big concert at the Crystal Palace last night left him just plain tuckered out."

"Ha!" The word exploded out of me, like a little pocket of anger in my chest had suddenly ignited and fired it off. "What's so tiring about showing off in front of a bunch of high-paying people who are clapping their hands off?''

I heard heavy footsteps coming toward us down the hallway, and immediately wished I'd kept my opinion to myself.

"Well, you see, little missy, it's not that simple," Burl drawled, lumbering like a bear into the small space where the hall emptied into the kitchen. He was blockaded by the boxes and sacks from coming any farther, so he stopped there, scratching his stomach with both hands. "It's like, the more high-paying the crowd, the harder they are to please. And the harder they are to please, the less prone they are to clap and the more prone they are to hurl insults and such at you."

Everybody was really super-quiet then.

"Eliza?" Mama said, her arms crossed and her mouth set funny.

"No offense, Burl," I murmured.

"None taken," Burl said, and laughed in a tired way. He sat down on the edge of a sturdy-looking box, then hopped back up when the box started to collapse. He looked heavier than before, and he wasn't even wearing a hat. Or his new hair. "And say, girls, I didn't mean to sound like our concert at the Palace last night was a flop. That is, I think with some sprucing up, a light show and a better sound system and such, our act will be more what they're expecting! Yessirree, it's not how you play, it's how you come across that counts."

"Sounds expensive," Dierdre said, and looked Burl in the eye. Her matter-of-fact way of talking came in handy sometimes. It was exactly what I was thinking but didn't have the nerve to say.

"Somewhat, yes," Burl agreed. "It'll require more of an investment, but I've got me a good woman who don't mind standing by me till the big payoff comes."

He winked at Mama, and she turned bright pink and looked down at her two pretty hands spread out on the table.

"Burl?" she said, and cleared her throat. "Uh, I guess I've recently made some . . . plans. That is, I don't see how I can invest in you boys any longer. I guess I'll be investing my time and energy and what little money I've got instead in . . . myself and in our friends here. You see, Hannah and I . . ."

She was interrupted by a knock at the door. We all had been listening so hard to Mama's speech that we were startled by the sound and all sort of jumped a little. Then Dierdre leaned across some boxes to shove the door open with her foot.

"Roger!" Mama exclaimed in a breathless way, jumping up from her chair.

Skeeter snatched off his baseball hat as he leaned into the room and gave Mama a shy smile. He noticed how crowded it was and stayed in the doorway, running his eyes over things.

"I can see you're busy in here," he said. His dark eyes stopped moving when he got to Burl. He clenched his jaw muscles a few times, then looked down at the hat in his hands. "I won't intrude. I just stopped by to say I've been

167

upstairs of the store building and done a little plumbing and such on the apartment up there. Might take a little painting's all, to get it looking really good."

Apartment? I mouthed to Dierdre, and she shrugged.

"Oh, Roger! You doll, you!" Mama cried then, rushing over to hug him. "What a sweetheart you are!"

Skeeter slowly brought his arms up, but Mama didn't notice and bounced out of his grasp to rush over and happily hug Hannah. She hugged me next, and over her skinny shoulder I watched Skeeter. His neck had turned a deep plum color and his eyes had a liquidy look as he glanced at Mama once more, then concentrated on putting on his hat.

"Just let me know when you're ready to move in," he said, his voice low and rumbly with embarrassment. "I'll come and bring whatever customers I've got to help you load up."

He reached over to leave something small and shiny on the cabinet, then glanced in an expressionless way at Burl, touched the brim of his hat and was gone. Mama hurried to the door and leaned out.

"Roger? Good-bye, and thank you, thank you, thank you a thousand times, you hear? Thank you, Roger. You doll!"

She shut the door and we all turned guiltily toward Burl, who hunkered there in the corner more than ever like a big, bewildered bear.

"Lorna Jean, would you mind telling me what in the

heck that was all about?'' he said in a loud, whiny voice, crossing his arms in a sulky way.

Mama picked up the key Skeeter had left and held it in both hands against her chest.

"Well, Burl, you see, last night at the auction Roger bought the old store building, and offered me the job of whipping it into shape and running it. And then, well, this morning after church he came over and told Hannah there was a little apartment upstairs of that building that she was welcome to, at least till Rick returns and they can make some better plans, since her house is, well, no longer with us, shall we say.''

She stopped, glanced sympathetically at Hannah, then bounced excitedly on her heels as she finished the story in a rush. "So we went up and looked at the apartment and it's plenty big enough for Hannah and me and the girls, so 'Wallah!' as they say in France, we are all four just up and moving over there!''

"Gosh dang,'' Burl whispered, shaking his head in confusion.

"I been thinking a lot here lately, Burl,'' Mama said quietly but firmly. "It seems to me there's two kinds of people that get tangled up into your life. One kind mostly sees you in terms of what you can do for them, such as making them look good in the eyes of other people and cooking for them when they take a notion to come home. And the other kind mostly sees what they'd like to do for you. And you don't mind a bit helping out the second kind, in fact that's enjoyment. But it gets mighty tiresome constantly helping out the first. Do you understand what I'm saying to you, hon? Understand why I'm leaving you?"

Burl frowned as though deep in thought, but finally shook his head sadly and sighed. "Lorna Jean, baby, I haven't got a clue."

"I know, Burl," Mama said wistfully. She worked her way across the cluttered little room to kiss his bald forehead tenderly. "You just plain haven't, baby."

She slipped past him and on down the hall, and we heard her softly close the bedroom door. Hannah, Dierdre, and I stared at Burl with a combination of sympathy and impatience. A couple of minutes later, he took the hint and made his way to the door.

"Good-bye, ladies," he said to us, scratching his head in a totally bewildered way, and left.

CHAPTER

~22~

Seconds after Burl shut the front door, Mama peeked
out of the bedroom, caught my eye and mouthed "Is he
gone?" I nodded and she hustled back into the kitchen
and began excitedly pulling cleaning supplies out of the
cabinets. Within half an hour the four of us crept from the
trailer like bandits, our arms filled with buckets, mops,
sponges, Ajax, and Lysol.

"I don't know why I feel so sneaky," Mama whispered
to Hannah, and giggled.

I couldn't figure it out either. We were only going to
clean up the apartment over the store, but it definitely felt
like the four of us were making some kind of getaway.

◆ ◆ ◆

The apartment turned out to be basically one huge
room with two tiny L-shaped rooms stuck on to the far
end of it like feet. One corner of the main room had been
turned into a kitchen, and one chink of the L-shaped
room that Hannah and Mama picked as their bedroom
had a teensy bathroom.

At one time, all the walls had evidently been covered with a design of wallpaper meant for kitchen use—a pattern of ivy and tea kettles on a light orange background. Part of that wallpaper was still clinging desperately to the walls, but most was in plastery, hardened-up globs on the floor.

Mama gave Dierdre and me the job of cleaning up those globs and mopping the floors while she and Hannah went back to the trailer and got things packed up for moving.

"We could possibly even spend this very night here!" she told us breathlessly, and Hannah nodded and smiled agreement in a pale, exhausted way. They went back down the rickety wooden stairway, Mama chattering happily but with a protective arm around Hannah's slumped shoulders. "When we've got this place all cleaned up and painted it's going to look so good I can hardly stand it!" was the last thing we heard her say as she cheerfully slammed the street-level door below us.

Sighing, I picked up a broom and garbage sack from the pile of cleaning supplies. "Want to sweep or hold the sack?" I asked, and Dierdre shrugged and reached for the broom.

We worked silently for quite a while, me on my knees holding the bag stretched open while she broomed junk into it. Then out of the blue, when we were finally almost finished, she stopped sweeping and said, "Eliza? What happened to your crystals?"

So she'd noticed the nearly empty, ring-stained windowsill after all. My heart skipped a beat. I didn't know your heart could really do that, but it did. Something about her voice told me she hadn't just casually noticed, either, but had noticed in a very big way.

"I just, you know, got tired of messing with them," I said in what I hoped was a nonchalant voice. "I . . . I'm giving them away. To a friend."

"What friend?"

"What friend what?"

"What friend is getting your crystals?"

I nudged at her tennis shoe with the sack, trying to get her to start brooming again, but she didn't. I gave up, and sat back on my ankles.

"Okay, Dierdre, if you must know, I'm giving my crystals to Lauren. As a gesture of friendship, because that's what friends do for other friends. They give them things. Like facials, or party invitations."

"Oh," she said, and began sweeping vigorously, scattering pieces of plaster and wallpaper gunk everywhere.

"Dierdre!" I quickly jerked the bag open, but still she made a mess, not aiming for the bag at all, even though I was clearly trying to hold it where the dirt was heading. In fact it was pretty clear that she was aiming that gunk right at *me!*

Finally I grabbed the broom from her and threw it across the room, furious at her for being so furious herself.

"What's so terrible about wanting to be friends with Amanda and Lauren and Casey anyway, Dierdre?" I yelled, jumping to my feet, breathing hard. Sweat ran

173

down my face in gritty-feeling streaks. "What's so terrible about trying to make a new life for myself, a better life? Will you answer me that, Dierdre, if you're so smart? When I look at them it's like there's this huge fist hitting me in the stomach over and over again with want! I want their stuff, Dierdre. Their perfect hair and cool clothes and . . . and different smiles for different occasions!"

Sweat was running down Dierdre's face too, puddling up in the deep pool-like spaces behind her collar bone. She walked over to where I'd thrown the broom, then snatched it up from the floor and stood clutching it with her back to me.

"I saw the Queen of England on TV once," she said, her voice fast and hollow and echoey in that empty room. "She was smiling kind of like Amanda smiles to people that aren't in her group. Her arm moved back and forth so evenly I wondered if it was real or if they'd invented a robotic arm for her that did her waving."

I waited for what seemed like hours for her to go on, then finally threw up my arms. "What's your point, Dierdre!"

She turned around, and her eyes had that red-rimmed look they sometimes got. "I don't think you need different smiles for different occasions, that's all. More than one smile confuses the issue and makes you wonder which one is real."

We just glared at each other then, across that shadowy room with its zillions of floating dust and plaster particles.

"Dierdre, listen . . ." I began, gulping.

"Just answer me one thing," she interrupted. "They're the candy bar you picked, right? And I'm the measles that you were just temporarily stuck with."

"Oh, Dierdre, can't you understand?" I pleaded. "This isn't anything personal against you! My makeover, giving Lauren my crystals, helping Amanda . . . borrow that encyclopedia—all of it's a start in that direction. In the direction of Richview Heights. You have to be in the right place with the right conditions around you if you want to grow into something beautiful! Crystals develop from the chemicals they're in! You can't grow a ruby in stupid old alum solution. Can't you see that?"

On the dirty floor, elm leaf shadows fidgeted restlessly, reaching for our ankles. A gust of humid, furnacy air poured into the room from the two big street-side windows, and a strange sound started up in the distance— faraway thunder.

"Can't you see that, Dierdre?" I repeated in a whisper.

"You told me that Amanda asked you to help her steal that encyclopedia. Well, why do you think she chose you to help, Eliza? You don't have to answer me, but you should answer yourself. Or better yet, if she's such a good friend, why don't you just ask her? Ask Amanda why she picked you to steal."

Her blunt demand fell like a boulder into the space between us.

"What?" I whispered, shaking my head. "Dierdre, I told you, it wasn't stealing! It was borrowing, and it's ancient history anyway because Amanda took that encyclopedia back days ago. And besides, I already figured out it was a friendship test, like sororities do."

"Then you shouldn't be afraid to just ask her," Dierdre said, snatching the pail and mop and stomping off to the bathroom to start noisily mopping.

I put my hands on my hips. I was so exasperated I was shaking. "I'm not afraid!" I called after her. "I'm just too polite to question her judgment! And if you didn't have such a science-book mind you'd understand about being polite like that, Dierdre! But you do, so you never, ever will!"

Then I grabbed the broom she'd dropped and furiously finished sweeping.

◆ ◆ ◆

An hour or so later Mama led a parade of men up the stairs with most of our stuff. The men were unsuspecting customers Skeeter had recruited, evidently, though they all seemed to be enjoying themselves as they worked, horsing around.

"We're borrowing the beds and kitchen table from the trailer, just for a little bit," Mama said three or four times to anyone who was listening. "I think that's only fair. And maybe we'll get a couple of chairs too, later. And a dresser or so."

She seemed to be astonished by the thoroughness of Dierdre's and my cleaning.

"I just can't believe how good a job you two did. Looks like a regular cleaning tornado has been through here!"

Dierdre and I stood tight-lipped and unsmiling in opposite corners of the big room. Mama looked puzzled for a second when neither of us said anything, then she turned and put a hand on my arm.

"Listen, honey, Hannah's taking a little rest at the trailer, but in a little bit I want you girls to go pack up the things in your room. We brought your clothes, but there was other stuff I didn't know if you wanted to keep or throw out."

I immediately stalked over to the stairs.

"I'll do it by myself!" I said, loud enough to be sure Dierdre heard. "I don't need anyone's so-called help."

♦ ♦ ♦

Hannah was sleeping soundly when I got inside the trailer, so I moved quickly and quietly. I put everything I wanted to keep in two grocery bags to take with me. I left the box of crystals I was taking to Lauren in the corner, figuring I could pick them up there to take them on the bus in the morning. Finally I threw some other small stuff, including the messy dud sapphire crystal jar, into a cardboard box which I placed next to the big overflowing metal garbage can behind the trailer.

♦ ♦ ♦

We did sleep in the apartment that night. Hannah was worried that Rick would come back and be frantic, wondering where she and Dierdre were, so she taped a note for him to the charred For Sale sign in their burned-out front yard.

There was a big window in our bedroom, and a rectangle of moonlight fell partly across Dierdre and partly across the wall behind her side of the bed. Occasionally the wind blew small black clouds through the sky, and their shadows skittered like spiders across Dierdre's sprawled, sleeping body, especially the leg and arm she had flung out from under the sheet for coolness.

How could she sleep with the gusty wind and the shadows? I myself couldn't fall asleep at all. I kept imagining that those shadow spiders were crawling off the wall and onto my pillow, then in through my ears to weave messy, tangled webs in my brain.

I tried thinking about the party I was invited to in Richview Heights, but Dierdre had messed up the soothing thrill of that with her suspicions. "Ask Amanda why she picked you to steal. Ask Amanda why she picked you to steal."

Finally I threw off my sheet and went to lean with my elbows on the windowsill. The stars throbbed over the soybean fields and Hilley's Woods. The cold creek threw up a mist as it crossed the heat-soaked road out of town, the one Rick must have taken. And Burl too, for that matter. The one the bus would take tomorrow morning with my crystal jars. Lauren's crystal jars.

The wind rose in a gust, pushing away a cloud that had covered the moon. A sudden beam of bright blue flared from the far edge of the window.

I bent toward that light and saw the sapphire crystal jar, purposely hidden behind a fold of the curtain.

Dierdre was so predictable. When she saw I'd come back from the trailer without the jar, she'd evidently gone to search for it herself. She'd retrieved it and put it in this far corner of the window where I wouldn't notice it and . . . what? Give it away to Lauren? Throw it in the trash again?

I picked up the jar, rotated it, and placed it in the middle of the sill. I knelt in front of it with my chin on my hands, squinting into its murky, mysterious depths.

"Poor dud sapphire," I whispered.

Thunder muttered from behind Hilley's Woods, triggering a chorus of howls from the coyotes. Behind my back, in the big front room, elm leaves scratched like restless fingernails against the screens in the windows. A monster storm was headed for us, all right.

I got back in bed, covered up with the sheet, and sealed the shadow spiders out of my ears with my hands. The last thing I noticed before I finally fell asleep was that the tea kettles on the torn wallpaper looked like witchy faces staring straight down at Dierdre.

CHAPTER
—23—

The sky was full of dark, greenish clouds when we got up the next morning, but it was still blisteringly hot. Hannah stayed in bed, and Dierdre, Mama, and I ate some cereal, sitting cross-legged on the kitchen floor. We hadn't gotten the table from Burl's trailer yet—stolen it, borrowed it, or whatever.

"Hannah cried in her sleep most of the night, poor thing," Mama whispered, leaning toward us confidentially. "I'm so worried about her. I wish Rick would come back from that fishing trip. None of the men in town even knows where he took off for, so they can't even find him to let him know about the fire."

Dierdre jumped up so fast her milk sloshed onto her leg. She thunked her bowl onto the counter and hurried out of the kitchen.

"What?" Mama asked.

I shrugged, stirring my corn flakes.

Mama put her own bowl down on the floor, scooted closer to me, and bent to look up into my face. "What,

Eliza? Did you girls have some kind of falling-out? Is that why you were acting so strange around each other last night?"

"She's just moody sometimes," I muttered.

Dierdre quietly reappeared in the kitchen doorway.

"I guess I won't go to school today," she said hoarsely, staring at the floor. "I think my mother needs me here."

Mama got up and went to hug her. "That's a good decision, hon," she said softly. "I'm sure she does."

◆ ◆ ◆

I lucked out and the bottom of the crystal box hadn't soaked completely through, though it did leave a murky puddle on the side of the bus seat where Dierdre used to sit.

At school, I knew the weight of the sloshing crystals made me look like I was waddling as I hustled down the hall, but there was nothing I could do about that. I headed right to the popular lockers, where luckily I caught Lauren and Amanda and Casey as they were grabbing out their books.

"Hi," I told Lauren. "I, you know, brought your crystals. Hope you like them."

Lauren peered into the box, frowning. "I don't get how to do these."

Amanda moved next to her and peered too. "Liza will come over tonight and show you," she said. "Right, Lisa?"

"Come over?" I asked breathlessly.

"Is her name Liza or Lisa?" Casey asked Amanda.

"Come over to Lauren's house," Amanda answered. "You can walk with us after school."

"You're inviting me to Richview Heights?" I asked, to be on the safe side.

The bell rang. Lauren slammed her locker. "You keep the crystals till this afternoon, okay? I don't have any place to keep them."

The three of them began hurrying down the hall. "Meet us at lunch and we'll make plans for this afternoon while we eat!" Amanda called back to me over her shoulder.

Today, you'll be going to Richview Heights after school, I told myself as a little trickle of chemical leaked from the soggy box and hit my sandal. "Today you'll be going to Richview Heights!" I said, quietly but out loud.

It didn't make me feel quite as excited as I thought it should have, probably because it had taken me by surprise.

♦ ♦ ♦

I decided I'd call home before lunch and make up some excuse for staying after school. In fact I waited behind two people to use the pay phone in the hall and had already raised my hand to start to dial before I remembered there was no phone in the new apartment.

Well, if I couldn't call, I couldn't call. When I didn't get off the bus Mama would eventually come looking for me at the school. I could get back to the school by then, and I definitely wouldn't have wanted her picking me up at Lauren's anyway. Not in Skeeter's gross little dentedup green car. Not when I wanted them all to think I lived on a luxurious ranch and Mama in her usual friendly, chatty way was sure to do something that would just scream out "Gouge Eye!"

Trying to call like that made me late, and the lunchroom line was long when I finally got there. I kept an eye on the popular table while I waited in line, but Amanda and those guys finished just before I was ready to sit down. Amanda caught my eye as they stood to leave, though, and shrugged and smiled a smile that seemed to mean she was sorry I had missed them.

Desperate, I moved toward the table where Dierdre usually sat. A bunch of girls were sitting there laughing together, but they got up and left without noticing me just as I got near. All of them, that is, but Nancy Petrinsen.

I sat down by Nancy. Anything was better than standing alone in the middle of the cafeteria, gawking around at the tables like you didn't have anybody to sit with.

"That stubble on your arms looks totally horrendous, Eliza," Nancy informed me.

◆ ◆ ◆

After English class I ran to my locker, knowing it would take a few minutes to pry the crystal box out since I'd had to really cram it in. If I didn't hurry, Amanda and Casey and Lauren might forget and leave without me.

But to my relief, they came up behind me and patiently slouched against the lockers across the hall as I eased out the box of sloppy chemical jars.

"Hi!" I greeted them with a nervous little laugh over

my shoulder as I put the squishy box down onto the tile floor. "I thought you guys might forget about me."

"No way," Lauren replied, and smacked her gum. "I need that stuff."

I turned quickly, anxious to see the expression on her face.

"And anyway we wouldn't forget you, Lisa," she said, smiling a dazzling smile. "You know that by now, right?"

"Sure," I answered, and turned, flustered, back to the box.

I could tell the cardboard bottom was quickly reaching the point of disintegration. The sides were also pretty soggy, from where the jars were all leaking slightly around the rims.

"Ready?" Amanda asked. She and Casey and Lauren began moving toward the side door of the school.

"Sure," I repeated, and stooped to pick up the messy box. Waddling again, I followed them down the hall.

◆ ◆ ◆

It was about a five-block walk to Richview Heights, which would have been like walking into paradise if the chemicals hadn't been sloshing me so bad, making the almost-healed scratches on my arms sting like crazy again. The houses on each block got bigger and bigger and farther apart, and the yards got greener and more planned-looking.

The entrance to Richview Heights was marked by a big open brick-and-iron gate. Inside that gate, each of the houses sprawled like a mermaid on its own green sea, cool and beautiful. There wasn't one sign of junk in any yard.

Lauren's house was made of yellow bricks and set on a hill, and behind it was a field bordered with a white wooden fence where two beautiful black horses ran. Not horses like in Gouge Eye, dusty and shaggy and snorting. These were jet black and sleek. Almost magical, like they might fly away at any moment.

"Your horses are gorgeous," I told Lauren.

"We can feed them some apples if you want," she said. "But it's pretty boring."

We walked to the front door, but Lauren stopped with her hand on the doorknob and looked me up and down.

"We better do the crystals outside on the deck. Mom hates coming home to messes."

On the deck off the side of Lauren's kitchen, I set up the chemicals while Amanda and Lauren and Casey went inside and got us Cokes. When they came back out and sat cross-legged beside me, I started explaining to Lauren about rotating the jars, though she kept jiggling her feet in a way that made me wonder if she was paying attention.

"Why's she have to do that rotating thing, anyway?" Casey asked. "The crystals are already done."

"They're not all that neat, though," Lauren said. "I thought you told us there'd be sapphires. Aren't they green? I mean, I expected more colors. There's just red and clear. How boring."

"Where are the green ones?" Casey asked, and looked at me. They all three looked at me, waiting.

"Well, actually, sapphires are blue," I said. "And,

well, there was just one. They're . . . tricky or something."

"So where's that one?" Amanda asked.

"Bring it tomorrow," Lauren said. "I was looking forward to more colors. Bring it, okay?"

"Let's go over to Amanda's and watch a movie," Lauren said, jumping to her feet. "It's going to rain outside here."

She ran down the deck stairs and started across the yard, with the others following close behind her.

"Wait! The jars!" I called, but nobody turned back around.

I quickly stuck the jars back inside the soggy box. I couldn't just leave the crystals out to get knocked over or messed up in the rain, but I wasn't supposed to go into Lauren's house. Not knowing what else to do, I clutched the box against my shirt and ran to catch up before I lost sight of Lauren, Casey, and Amanda. The beautiful horses watched me expectantly, their heads over the fence, probably hoping for those apples.

◆ ◆ ◆

Amanda lived just two houses down, in a red brick house that looked exactly like a small castle. It even had a turret room—round with a cone-shaped roof.

Touching the front of my T-shirt to see if it had dried, Amanda said, "Put that crystal box down here on the porch. We can go inside if you're careful not to lean against anything."

The second floor of the little turret turned out to be

Amanda's bedroom. It was beautiful but messy, yellow and white with lots of ruffles on the curtains and canopy bed. Casey and Lauren kicked their shoes off and went to sprawl on their stomachs in the part of the room where a VCR and TV shared a bookcase near Amanda's bed. Amanda's thick white carpeting was soft as a cloud. In fact, the whole room seemed a lot like a sloppy version of heaven.

"Come on," Casey said to me over her shoulder, so I joined them, but sat carefully on the carpet instead of lying on my stomach, since I was trying not to lean on anything.

Amanda switched on the TV, took out a movie from a stack of tapes on her bookcase and fed it to the VCR, then sank down beside us. She reached over and pulled a bag of chips from under her bed, and they all three began automatically munching while the words warning you not to copy the movie crawled slowly by.

Since their eyes were on the movie, I ran my own eyes over everything in the wonderful room. There was a stereo system with two huge speakers, and beside that a cabinet with boxes of compact discs. Beyond that, the double closet stood bulging open, shoes cluttering the floor like a fleet of tiny, bright boats.

There were stacks of beauty magazines on the bookcase with the VCR tapes. On the bottom shelf, Amanda had let an assortment of snack dishes and glasses accumulate. And in the corner of that bottom shelf, the library's

"O" encyclopedia was smashed under a small plate with half a peanut butter sandwich on it. The encyclopedia was open and a few pages were folded back, held down under a sticky-looking glass of something orange.

CHAPTER
~24~

Rock music from the movie began thumping through the room, but I heard it like you'd hear something from deep under water. The thing drowning it out was the sound of my own blood, surging in fast, fuzzy waves against the inside of my eardrums.

"What's she looking so weird about anyway?" I heard Casey ask. At first I thought she was talking about somebody in the movie, then I realized she meant me.

I turned toward Amanda. "Didn't you take the encyclopedia back?" I was so stunned that the words just sort of rushed out of me before I even knew what I was saying.

She looked at me, then looked at Lauren and rolled her eyes. "Duh! I guess not, since it's still here." They all three laughed fast, sharp laughs, then Lauren put her finger to her lips and said, "Quiet! Here comes the good part where he kisses her."

"But I mean, why not?" My heart was racing and it was hard to talk normally, but if there was a good reason, I needed more than anything in the world to know it and to know it right that second.

They were all three staring at the long, slow kiss on the TV screen, though, and ignoring me.

I crawled quietly over to the bookcase and moved the sticky glass. There was a deep wet ring through several of the pages under it. I wiped the worst of that off, unfolded the bent pages, smoothed them, and closed the heavy book to keep them straight.

"Amanda?" I squeezed shut my eyes, then forced them open and turned back toward where she was sprawled on the carpet. "Listen, uh . . . I'll take the encyclopedia back tomorrow, okay?"

She immediately sat up, wrapped her arms around her knees, and swiveled in my direction, frowning. "Why would you want to do that? You could get us both in trouble!"

"Don't worry," I said, and tried to smile, "I won't tell Miss Coates you were the one who took it."

Her mouth dropped open. Her gum was a startling pink blob on her tongue. "Me? I DIDN'T take it! Hey, you took it, Lisa!"

"Yeah, Lisa," Casey said, without moving her eyes from the movie.

I grabbed the encyclopedia. It started to slide through my sweaty fingers, so I hugged it to my chest and locked my arms across it. There was no way in the world I could have stopped Dierdre's matter-of-fact voice from hammering through my brain as I got to my knees, then clumsily to my feet. *Ask Amanda why she picked you to steal . . . why she picked you to steal.*

"Okay, but why . . ." I swallowed and licked my lips.

"Amanda!" Lauren whined. "Turn around! Watch this!"

It was now, or never. "Why did you ask me to take it?" I forced out. "Why did you . . . pick me?"

"You were wearing that bulky sweater, remember?" Amanda said, with an irritated shrug. "And besides, you'd sort of almost lied to Mrs. Hogelman about not doing your paper, so I figured you'd do this, too."

"Then Dierdre was right!"

I didn't realize I'd said that out loud, but I heard Lauren ask Casey, in a loud whisper, "Dierdre? Isn't she that geeky smart kid with the hair that's even weirder than Lisa's?"

The cloud carpet felt like it was moving beneath my feet, and my stomach started churning. In what seemed like slow motion, Amanda stood and started walking toward me, shaking her head. She stretched out long, rubbery-looking fingers and tried to yank the encyclopedia from my arms, but I clutched it more tightly, and she looked shocked.

"I can't believe this!" she yelled, turning toward the others.

"Lisa, come on, lighten up!" Casey said over her shoulder. "Nobody will ever want that stupid encyclopedia anyway. I mean, the library must have about a jillion of them."

When Amanda turned back toward me, she was smiling again, this time ultra-sweetly. "Hey, Casey's right. But still, I'll take it back myself if it means that much to you. Okay?" She took ahold of the top of the encyclopedia and began jerking it as she talked, one tug for each word. "Just *give–it–to–me.*"

With each of her tugs, I took a little step backward, clutching the encyclopedia for dear life.

"I can't." My ears were ringing and my stomach churned harder.

"What do you mean, you can't? Just hand it over!"

"I mean I can't . . . can't trust you. You're smiling at me, but I can't tell which of your smiles you're using, a real one, or a fake one!"

I turned then and stumbled blindly along the cloud carpet until I was out of Amanda's room and scrambling down the stairs. She started after me, yelling at me to stop, but when I reached her front door I wrenched it wide open, plunged through and grabbed a jar from the box on her little front porch. Then I jumped back into the doorway, holding that crystal jar out and up in my right hand, like a grenade.

"Back off!" I yelled, crushing the encyclopedia to me with my left arm so it felt kind of like a shield. "Unless your mother likes her front room decorated with chemical crust, Amanda, you'd all three just better go back upstairs and leave me alone!"

Amanda immediately backed away, holding her hands up in front of her. "Just get out of here," she said, her eyes wide and fastened on that drippy crystal jar I was holding over her mother's fancy purple carpet.

"She's crazy," Casey added from partway up the stairs, looking like she was finally more interested in real life than the movie.

Lauren said something too, but I didn't hear what it was. I was out on the porch again by then, busy cramming the jar back into its spot, balancing the encyclopedia on top of the jars, snatching up the whole soggy mess, and trying hard not to cry.

When I ran from the house, they didn't follow.

◆ ◆ ◆

I was just past Lauren's house when the bottom of the box finally gave way and the crystal jars smashed into smithereens all over the brick sidewalk. I was crying pretty hysterically by then, just really all-out sobbing since no one was watching, so it was hard to see well enough to push the shards of glass and broken crystal to the edge of the grass. Still, I tried. I didn't want any little kid stepping on that mess before a grown-up cleaned it up. Lauren's horses watched me. They seemed sympathetic and sad, and seeing that, I cried even harder—loud, jerky sobs that sounded like "Uh-huck, uh-huck! Uh-*huck!*"

One of the horses suddenly whinnied, stomped the ground, and tossed his mane. I looked at him, then looked where he was looking, up at the sky. Something very weird was happening. The greenish clouds that had hung close and stifling all day were moving now, boiling. Lightning fluttered in all directions, moving behind and through those clouds like a hundred beating hearts.

"Mama!" I yelled. I picked up the encyclopedia and began running again, full-speed. Tiny splinters from the jar were caught under the straps of my sandals and bit at my feet. "Mama, where are you? Uh-huck, uh-huck."

I sped through the gates of Richview Heights, down the sidewalks that got more crumbly and grass-cracked as they led to the school. Then finally I saw the school itself in the distance, flickering with lightning so that for half a second I actually thought some Jay Roy type had realized a long-bragged-about dream and was blowing it up.

"Mama!" I screamed. "Uh-*huck!* Mama!" Would she even be able to find me, since she didn't know where I was? I forced myself to calm down enough to listen. Everything was eerily quiet, as though the air itself was holding its breath. Then I suddenly heard the popping rumble of Skeeter's rusted-out tailpipe, and the little green Volkswagen came barreling around the corner of the school, looking like a shimmering, iridescent beetle in the weird light.

"Mama, here I am!" I screeched, jumping up and down.

The beetle gave a sudden lurch, then came racing toward me like it was being chased by a spider. The instant Mama came to a rolling stop, I jumped in and leaned across the gearshift knob to throw my arms around her neck.

"I'm sorry, I'm sorry, I'm sorry," I sobbed into her wild, beautiful hair. "Go ahead and bawl me out."

But she took her foot off the gas so the car died with a big, shaky belch, then she hugged me tight right back.

"Oh honey, oh sweetheart, I was so afraid when I couldn't find you, because I love you so much and I don't know how I could survive it if you up and disappeared on me." She pushed me away then, grabbing my arms above the elbows and looking into my eyes. "Eliza, where were you anyway? Where?"

I swallowed. "It's . . . it's a long story," I croaked.

To my surprise and relief she left it at that, and hugged me again, and suddenly she was crying every bit as hysterically as I was. "Eliza, this has been a just awful day. Just awful! You know that old falling down shed where Rick kept his ax and saws in the back corner of their property?"

I pushed away from her enough to see her face, but before I could even nod, she went on in a rush. "Well, this afternoon Hannah took a notion to go look inside that shed, to see if she could find a clue as to where Rick might be. And the whole shed was jam-packed with her and Dierdre's clothes and other little things which were valuables to them, most for sentimental reasons. Like the old chiming clock Hannah'd inherited from her mother. Honey, Rick set the fire himself! He shoved that stuff into the shed to save it! He must have known Hannah would realize he did it when she saw the inside of the shed, but

I guess he felt no one but her would have to be the wiser and she could file for insurance money. I can't believe he didn't know her better than that. Hannah doesn't have a dishonest bone in her body, and now that she knows it was arson, not just an accident, she wouldn't think of trying to cheat and file a claim. So the fire was for nothing. Nothing! Nothing but a big old two-ton load of grief."

She dug a soggy glob of tissues from the Juanita pocket of her waitressing uniform, honked her nose, and started the car.

"And honey, the worst part. Just inside the door of the shed there was a word spelled out in the dust of the floor. Dierdre took one look at that word and ran, and we haven't seen her since. We need to get back and take care of them, pronto. You need to find Dierdre, if you can, before this awful storm breaks."

"But what was the word scratched in the dust?"

Mama slammed both fists down once, hard, on the steering wheel. I flinched—it was the only time in my life I'd seen her actually hit anything in anger.

"The word Rick left behind him was . . . was 'Sorry'! He breaks the hearts of people that love him, then has the nerve to leave behind a little old nothing of a one-word apology. He lets his family's trust in him go up in smoke, then thinks a little dusty word will help."

She looked in my eyes as she floored the gas pedal, barely missing a speed limit sign when the right front tire went over the curb. "Now isn't that about the most pathetic thing you ever heard of?" she called above the motor and tire and exhaust noise.

I didn't answer. I was thinking of a different pathetic word, the word "measles." *They're the candy bar you picked,* Dierdre had said, *and I'm the measles you were just temporarily stuck with.*

CHAPTER

~25~

Mama drove fast and kept looking worriedly out the windows. She switched on the staticky, nearly hopeless radio to try and hear the weather reports. The thunder mumbled constantly now, and every couple of minutes it let loose with a tooth-rattling *kaboom,* as though the mumbler in the clouds felt ignored and was hurling cherry bombs to get everyone's attention.

". . . fughkrrul crahld heading east-northeast at cruigly-grive miles an hour," the radio crackled. "Persons in the crockeskreene and rockwesene vicinity should take skeeesher immediatekrrry!"

"Did they say 'funnel cloud'?" Mama asked breathlessly, her face pale. "Did they say to take shelter?"

"I think," I said. "But maybe they weren't talking about us."

"Maybe," she said doubtfully, licking her lips.

The trees were nodding, wildly and merrily, as if they were trying to add their two cents worth and say, "Oh, yes, they are *so* talking about you!"

"Step on it," Mama told herself, and floored the gas pedal. Skeeter's green bug butted its little snub nose bravely into the wind, and before I knew it, the green bullet hole–speckled "Gouge Eye, Missouri, population 435" sign loomed ahead of us, the most beautiful thing I'd ever seen.

KEEE-RACKK!! The sky seemed to rip as a skeleton finger of lightning reached out of the clouds and touched the red light on top of the elevator tower.

"Almost home," Mama whispered, careening around the corner and onto Gouge Eye's main road, "and not a single tiny little second too soon."

But a crowd of worried-looking people was gathered on the small porch outside Skeeter's as we pulled up to the apartment. "What?" Mama yelled across to them through the howl of the wind, and Hannah separated herself from them and ran over to us.

"Dierdre's still gone! My baby! We've all been looking. Skeeter and some other men have searched at the creek where the kids play in the summer. Now they're out in B.J.'s truck looking along the road to Branson. Oh, Lorna Jean!"

She grabbed Mama, and I turned and dashed into the store building and on upstairs to put on better shoes for running. My heart was slamming, but still I knew Dierdre had to be on the raft. The men just hadn't looked upcreek, toward the cave, that was all. Or maybe Dierdre had seen them and hidden, for some reason. That's where she had to be, though. She had to!

I threw the encyclopedia onto the bed, kicked off the flimsy sandals I'd worn to school, and pulled on my tennis shoes. My shaking fingers felt like crayons as I rushed, tying my laces. *Calm down, calm down.* She was probably on her way home right now, and I'd meet her halfway through the soybeans with her nose in that silly notebook of hers, too caught up in recording measurements to even notice how bad the weather had gotten as she'd dangled on her raft in the current.

Lightning struck somewhere close outside the bedroom window, a flash of sudden screeching light that turned the white shoe I was tying blue.

Blue light? I glanced quickly over my shoulder. The sapphire on the windowsill had finally pulled itself together into a real, solid gem. It was absorbing what was left of the light and glowed brilliantly as the clouds swirled beyond it.

And then I noticed something else, and froze.

There was a slip of paper caught under the edge of the sapphire jar.

I sped across the room, grabbed up the jar, and snatched the note. "Be sure to rotate this twice a day," it said.

"Deeer-drah!" I screamed, leaning out the window toward the distant creek. Then, still holding the jar, I stumbled down the stairs and past our mothers, ignoring what they shouted as I ran on toward the soybean field.

Dierdre's flat, quiet words the night of the fire banged

through my head, and as I ran I finished the sentence I hadn't had the nerve to let her finish then. *I built the raft . . . I mostly built the raft . . . to escape with!*

Dierdre wasn't coming back!

Dierdre actually planned to cut the raft free of its tether rope. She'd probably even done that by now!

Dierdre was headed toward the Mississippi River! Or, more probably, to a wipeout on the sharp rocks and fast rapids below the highway bridge.

"Deeer-drah!"

The lightning was constant beyond Hilley's Woods as I ran like I had never run before through the waving, dancing soybeans. Constant as an explosion in a fireworks factory. Constant as the place in my heart where my dad would always live, whether I'd told him good-bye or not. Dierdre hadn't said good-bye either, to her father or to me. I *knew* she might do something like this! I *knew*, but I hadn't wanted to let myself face the fact that I knew.

Friends weren't like candy bars *or* measles. They were like shots—you got the ones you needed whether you thought you needed them or not and no matter how much they hurt.

Don't think, don't think! Just run!

"Deeer-drah!" I screamed, plunging into the woods, tripping and tangling as I ran through the thick, leafy overgrowth. I was out of breath but couldn't take time to get it back.

At some point I noticed the crystal jar in my hand. Still

running, I unscrewed the lid and all the chemicals immediately slopped out onto my pants and shoes. I yanked the
crystal string loose from the lid and dropped the jar.

The bluff arose from the path in front of me, glowing
like an emerald in the greenish light, blocking most of the
wind, which howled and screeched like a banshee around
its craggy edges.

There was the sycamore tree! And there was the tether
rope wrapped around its wide, blotchy trunk. As I'd
known it would be, the raft was gone from the bank. In
seconds I would be able to see the other end of the rope,
drifting loose in the current where Dierdre had cut it with
that ax of hers so she could float free.

I crashed through the last small trees and teetered,
buffeted by the swirling wind, dizzy with fear and dread,
on the steep bank of the creek.

"Dierdre?" I whispered, and forced myself to raise my
eyes to look at the limp rope in the horrible, empty water.

But the water wasn't empty. Dierdre was sitting cross-
legged on the still-tethered raft out there as it tossed with
the current.

"Dierdre!" My knees buckled with relief, and I toppled
and slid down the muddy bank and right into the edge of
the water.

She turned her head slowly and looked at me, expressionless. Then she looked back at the water and began
talking, calmly and in that low, flat voice of hers. The
steep creek banks blocked the wind and it was eerily quiet

there on the water, though I still had to strain to hear her as I tried to splash to my feet on the slick rocks.

"When I was little, Daddy told me stories of a magic, giant white trout that lives in Twisted Creek," she said, talking more to the water tumbling in front of her than to me. "The Trout King lives where the creek runs really cold and deep, in Sink Cave. If you make it past Sink Cave, then Twisted Creek runs into the Missouri River, then the Missouri meets the . . ."

"I know, I know, the Mississippi. Dierdre, quit talking like that and come to shore!" I ripped off my shoes, ignored the fact that they floated away, and tried to balance for the fourth or fifth time. My bare toes finally gripped the mossy rocks and I waded out a little closer to her. "I know you're feeling rotten, Dierdre, but come to shore so we can talk about it. Lightning hit the elevator a while ago. Water's not good in lightning. Dierdre? Come on in. Please?"

She turned to me again, and this time I could see wide tear tracks down the sweaty dirt on her face. "I can possibly make it down the big rapids, Eliza. I've done tests, made little stick rafts and sent them down. They occasionally make it, and this is one solid raft. You said so yourself, remember?"

The sky split open behind us and filled with dynamite.

"Dierdre!" I yelled. "Occasionally isn't good enough when we're talking about possibly drowning! Now come in, and I mean it, before we're both electrocuted!"

But she just stood up, using the long pole to balance with, and moved toward the back of the raft. There she crouched down by the rudder, and for the first time I noticed a glint and saw her ax lying on the logs near her feet.

I kicked off then and swam through the icy water. When I reached the raft I pulled with all my might and hefted myself clumsily onto it, shaking all over.

"Dierdre, luh . . . listen to me," I said, my teeth rattling with cold and fear. "I did what you said. I asked Amanda why she picked me, and she said because she knew I'd steal. I wouldn't have asked her if it wasn't for you."

Her back was to me, but I saw her left arm reach out and pick up the ax. "Swim to shore, Eliza," she said quietly.

"Dierdre! Dierdre, sorry is an awful word. What's it mean, anyhow? On the other hand, sometimes people really are. Sorry, that is. I've . . . I've never gotten very close to anyone my age before. I didn't know it got so complicated. I thought loyalty was something I saw in Winstead's sometimes. Shopping together and parties and stuff. Dumb, huh? Now I know it's a thing you do, a thing you give back to someone when they give it to you. Let's pole back to shore and talk about all this stuff, okay?"

Her elbows stopped moving, but still she didn't face me.

"Okay, think of this," I said, clutching my arms to keep from shaking apart as I knee-walked cautiously forward and came up right behind her. "Maybe after you cut that rope and sail free into this storm you'll come upon the big, white, magic Trout King. And maybe you'll hop on his back and ride him down Sink Cave, Dierdre, clear to the center of the earth. And maybe it'll be glittering and beautiful as a ruby crystal down there, but . . . *but maybe it'll be so icy and sharp your eyeballs will explode out of you like popcorn!*"

That took her by surprise and, like I'd hoped she would, she swiveled her head around toward me, frowning in confusion.

"Look!" I exclaimed, opening my hand and dangling the sapphire crystal in front of her. "You did it, Dierdre. You wouldn't give up on it even when it was clearly a dud, and you finally made it come together. It's beautiful, isn't it? But you have to make a choice, right this second."

I closed my hand around the crystal and moved my arm out over the water. "One thing goes overboard, into the water. Drop the ax, Dierdre, or I drop the sapphire crystal."

"Don't!" Dierdre yelled.

"Then drop that ax!" I yelled back, letting the sapphire slide from my palm to dangle over the water from its tiny string, now wrapped around my finger. "Now, Dierdre! Drop it by the count of three or the sapphire's history! One, two . . ."

The ax hit the water and sank like a stone. Actually, probably even faster than a stone, being heavy iron and all.

I had never been so shocked and relieved in my life. My

trade-off idea had been a desperate, last-second move, and I hadn't really expected it to work. Dierdre had planned this escape for so long—who'd have dreamed she'd choose the crystal?

She stared at the water where the ax had disappeared for a few seconds, then, without looking me in the eye, got to her feet and picked up the pole.

I was limp and shaky, but somehow I managed to stand up beside her. I held out the sapphire, she took it and slipped it into her pocket, then we both put our weight against the pole. Without talking, we moved the raft slowly but steadily through the churning water, to shore.

CHAPTER
—⚬ 26 ⚬—

The Civil Defense siren in Gouge Eye blasted out a tornado warning while we were running toward home through the woods. Skeeter and B. J. had given up driving around looking for us and now were keeping a lookout with our mothers from the bell tower of the church. When they spotted us thrashing through the wind-whipped soybeans, they all four rushed to us and pretty much dragged us along that last block or so, faster than we could have run against the wind with our own legs by then. We all got pummeled by golfball-sized hailstones. A bunch of people who had gathered to ride out the storm in the basement of the church threw open the big double basement doors and yanked us inside just in the nick of time.

"You girls took twenty years off our lives!" Mama and Hannah exclaimed several times, together and separately. The wind was too loud, even inside the church basement, for talking by then, but they more or less screamed in our ears. "I don't know whether to hug you or wring your neck!" was another thing I remember one of our mothers screeching. Then the wind came up even harder, and Mama nearly broke a bunch of my ribs, hugging me close as an invisible freight train ripped along tracks in the sky right over our heads.

◆ ◆ ◆

We stayed clenched together like that for minutes or hours—time is a thing that doesn't work right in a tornado, so who knows? And finally that sky train passed on, dragging the heat of the past weeks like a ragtag caboose behind it. The birds began making a few careful stabs at singing, sharp chirps which sounded like confused complaints about the damage done to their trees. The excited coyotes howled like crazy in the woods.

There in the basement, people cautiously stood from where they'd hunkered down against the walls. Everyone looked a little dazed. The first people to try talking talked too loud at first, then laughed at themselves. We couldn't believe how quiet it was now that the wind had stopped.

We had to pick our way carefully outside, even after a few of the men had cleared things away from the big concrete basement stairs. By the light of a glowing fall sunset we saw piles and piles of broken tree limbs mixed with bricks and twisted metal and glass.

It turned out that the tornado hopscotched right over the big, flashy target of Branson, missing it altogether. But it nicked Gouge Eye, and in a town of 435 people, a nick amounts to a lot.

The gas station was gone, had just been picked delicately off the side of the elevator like somebody would pick an apple from its tree. The Civil Defense siren was warped, as though it had told a secret when it warned people about the tornado and the tornado had swiped at it for punishment. Burl's old trailer was just plain flattened like a squashed pink balloon. All of the ancient, two-story buildings downtown, including the store building and Skeeter's, were missing a few bricks from their top stories, and had lots of windows blown out. The For Sale sign in front of the charred ruins of Dierdre's house had blown away, and the already cracked red light on top of the elevator was blasted to smithereens.

The six orange pig feeders in front of Heckleman's Lumberteria were still there, in exactly the place they always have been and will, I predict, always be.

◆　◆　◆

Skeeter, Mama, Hannah, Dierdre, and I hurried up to the apartment over the store building. Things had been tossed around up there and soaked from the wind and water coming in the broken windows. New globs of the teakettle wallpaper were hanging loose and balled up with broken glass all over the floor.

"Well," Mama said, and took a deep breath. "Well."

Then she shook back her hair, clapped her hands and laughed out loud. "Say, isn't it just the luckiest thing we hadn't started painting yet? I tell you, things do just work out for the best in life, now don't they?"

Skeeter grinned and looked at her like he wanted to grab her and hold on to her forever. I decided right then and there I would make an effort to call him Roger.

I walked past where Dierdre and her mother stood like pale ghosts at the top of the stairway, their heads close together. Hannah's short, plump arm was stretched up and around Dierdre's tall, skinny shoulders.

I walked on into our bedroom.

The window in our room hadn't been broken—it was on the wrong side of the building for that. Outside that window, things looked sharper and greener than I'd ever seen them in Gouge Eye, with the haze of heat and humidity gone.

I heard a sound and turned to see Dierdre standing right behind me in our doorway. She was scraping at a loose hunk of wallpaper with her thumbnail, frowning at it.

"Did you mean that, out on the creek?" she asked hoarsely, still frowning at her thumbnail. "About loyalty and stuff?"

I walked over to the bed and picked up the warped and chemical-crusty book that was lying there. "Here," I said, handing it to Dierdre. "It's the stolen encyclopedia. I'm taking it back to Miss Coates and facing the consequences. When I saw it there in Amanda's room and asked her that question you told me to ask her, it was like . . . it was like things had been swirling around inside me for a long, long time, and they suddenly just came together into something solid and I . . . remembered . . ."

"You remembered what?" she asked.

I swallowed. "I remembered who I was, before. I was nobody's slave, nobody's thief. The me my dad was proud of was just . . . herself. Then he died, and I guess I couldn't face being me because I hurt so bad and I was so scared, so I just kind of . . . hid. The thing is, Dierdre, I guess I hid myself so well that even I couldn't find me, until today. I owe you a lot for not, you know . . . giving up on me."

Dierdre slid down till she was sitting on the floor, then she opened the encyclopedia on her lap and began riffling through the pages. "If you want, I'll go with you to talk to Miss Coates," she offered.

"Thanks," I said, and felt a surge of relief.

She closed the encyclopedia, and a little sparkling shower of chemicals puffed out of it like fairy dust. "I owe you, too," she said, staring down at her long fingers, spread across the cover of that ruined book. "I was out on the raft for a long time this afternoon. And I kept looking over at the bank, and finally it dawned on me that I was hoping you'd suddenly be standing there." She looked up at me. "Eliza, I think way deep inside I knew it was too dangerous to cut that tether, and I was hoping you'd come and make me go home."

I held out my hand. "Give me the sapphire," I said.

She dug in her pocket, and handed it to me. I walked

211

over and hung it by its string from the little iron lock at the top of the window. The setting sun immediately hit it and filled the room with dancing blue spangles.

We both caught our breath. Dierdre got to her feet and we held out our arms and spun around and around like silly little toddlers, laughing as the light painted our clothes and hands and hair. We finally fell down, dizzy from spinning and slaphappy from the day's excitement.

Dierdre breathed a deep sigh and said, "I didn't realize how much I've been worrying about the Mississippi. I'm just so relieved it's gone!"

I raised up on one elbow and squinted at her. "You're relieved the Mississippi is gone?"

"No, the ax!" She looked puzzled. "Why would I be glad the Mississippi is gone? After all, it's the largest river in the nation, and second in the world."

I shook my head, smiling but rolling my eyes.

"Well, it is," she said, and shrugged.

Dierdre has a brain-strain science-book mind.

You get used to it.

EPILOGUE

 $\mathbf{M}$ r. Amos can read and write! Sort of, at least. Yesterday, October 1, I got a letter from him.

When I went to pick up Mama's mail, Miss Cleaver took it from our cubbyhole at the post office and handed it to me.

"Ta-dum!" she said, with a big smile she must save for the first time you get your own personal mail. At first I didn't recognize the name in the top left corner of the envelope.

"Thaddeus T. Amos?" I asked.

Miss Cleaver sadly shook her head and shrugged. She'd evidently already spent some time running possibilities through her mind, and had come up blank.

And then it dawned on me. "Mr. Amos!" I yelled, and Miss Cleaver looked relieved and smiled. "Oh, good," she said. "That's settled, then."

I rushed outside into the sunshine and ripped open the envelope, and a baseball card fluttered out like a butterfly and landed on my shoe. I picked it up and could hardly believe my eyes—a George Brett rookie card! After carefully putting it in my T-shirt pocket, I pulled out the folded piece of notebook paper that was also in the envelope. It said:

> *Dear Eliza,*
>
> *I have exciting news! I can read somewhat and am experiencing improvement every day! I can also write, though my volunteer adult literacy tutor at Johnson County Community College, Ms. Creneth-Tate, is taking down this letter from my dictation. One day soon, though, you will be receiving letters from my own hand!*
>
> *Won't that be just fine? I can't wait, can you?*
>
> > *Yours sincerely,*

I had to squint really hard to read the rest. Up till "sincerely," the letters were round and in dark purple ink, but beneath that the writing was in smeary pencil and the letters were printed and sort of wobbly-looking. I easily read the signature, Thaddeus, since I knew from the envelope what to expect. The two lines under that took me a lot longer. I finally made out, "Ms. C-T bigshot is stiff but o.k. and teaches me good. How bout that, me reading huh? Rite back, here? I be able to read it now. The rookie card for good luck."

"Rite back, here?" I finally figured out didn't mean "right back here," but meant, "Write back, hear?"

So today, October 2, I did. I took all afternoon and did it right. The letter was so fat when I finished that Miss

Cleaver, acting apologetic, told me it needed an extra stamp.

Dear Mr. Amos,

Boy, was I glad to get your letter, even though I could tell the first part wasn't exactly you talking. I wrote you twice, a long time ago, but the letters were too whiny to mail.

A lot has happened here. You were right—this move to Gouge Eye has been an adventure. The people next door had a fire, and Burl's trailer was crunched in a tornado. Now our neighbors, the fire girl (who's my best friend, Dierdre) and her mother, and Mama and me live in an apartment together upstairs from a grocery store Mama is soon going to be running. Burl is out of the picture, and a cool, princelike guy named Roger is in.

Here's something funny that happened. You'll laugh. About a week after the tornado, there were suddenly flies all over town, jillions of them swarming everywhere. There was also an obnoxious smell. Reverend Hartsill called it a "true pestilence" which got all the grown-ups worked up. Then we discovered B. J. Turley had decided to go on vacation before he started fixing up the damage to his building, and he accidentally left 12 dozen eggs in his bank safe! After those rotten eggs were buried at the dump, our "pestilence" was over. Dierdre and I still crack up ("crack up," get

*it?) whenever anybody mentions eggs. I told you
you'd laugh.*

*See what I mean? I repeat: A LOT HAS HAP-
PENED!!*

*School is good. Dierdre and I sit with some girls
at lunch who are getting to be our friends. They
like Dierdre's smartness. Some people think that
kind of thing is cool in junior high. One of them is
sort of obnoxious, but I'm learning to live with it.*

*Dierdre built a raft and takes wind and water
measurements. Someday I'll tell you more about
the raft. You would love it. It took first place in
our science fair. I put together a last-minute rock
collection that got a C and didn't place. Oh, well.
I'm also working in the public library three after-
noons a week after school. I'm paying for something. It's a long story. I'll tell you all about it in
another letter.*

*Don't think that because I haven't mentioned it
yet I don't ABSOLUTELY LOVE the George
Brett card. I do! I LOVE IT!! I'll carry it always
for luck, and to remind me of the good times we
had trading cards and playing rummy and just
plain talking last summer.*

*One more thing—I made the crystals from that
kit my dad bought me. Remember? I told you about
that kit once. Anyway, the alums and rubies came
out okay, but the sapphire is truly unique. Dierdre
and I keep it in our window and share it, since she*

helped me grow it. Actually, I'd say we grew it together, fifty-fifty. Don't let anyone tell you that growing a crystal garden is easy. It's not! It's very, very tricky, even with a kit, and there are about a jillion ways to mess up. It was worth it, though, because, boy, did I learn a lot.

Well, gotta go. Write me back. I'll write you back.

Your friend forever, Eliza.

When I finished writing all that, my hand felt like it was about to fall off. Smiling to myself as I thought of how Mr. Amos would chuckle when he read about those rotten eggs, I folded the letter and put it in an envelope. Dierdre walked with me to the post office, and we bought that extra stamp and sent my fat letter on its way.